MW01200207

# BEHIND *the* GLASS

State Street Series: Book 1

# Behind the Glass

## Kristen Morgen

Tamarind Hill Press

www.tamarindhillpress.co.uk

First edition published in 2014

Second edition published in February 2020

Copyright © 2020 Tamarind Hill Press
London, United Kingdom

The moral right of Kristen Morgen to be identified as
the author of this work has been asserted in
accordance with the Copyright, Design and Patents
Act of 1988.
All rights reserved. No part of this publication may be
reproduced, stored in a retrievable system, or
transmitted in any form or by any means, electronic,
mechanical photocopying, recording or otherwise,
without the permission of the author and copyright
owner.

Cover Design by Marianne Nowicki

ISBN
978-1-64786-392-0

**TAMARiND HiLL**
**.PRESS**

# THANK YOU

*It has been a long journey. Writing the first edition of this book, being a published author, and learning the remarkable business of the book world has been an incredible experience.*

*As I embark on the biggest stage of my journey, partnering with Tamarind Hill Press with the second edition of Behind the Glass, I want to thank everyone who made my book a success since its initial publication in 2014.*

*I can't adequately express how happy and excited I am at the response to my debut novel. There really is nothing more rewarding than reading a review of the book you poured your heart and soul into. If my writing connects with readers in even the smallest way and helps them see things in their own lives differently, that is honestly the most amazing thing in the world. Being able to touch another human being through my words is why I love being an author.*

*The success of this book, along with the many wonderful five-star reviews it's gotten over the years, are only possible because of you. Thank you to my readers, my followers, my awesome literary community, and my friends and family for your constant support! Mere words can't adequately*

i

express the endless gratitude I feel toward everyone who has supported me and my book since its first publication. It truly means the world to me!

For those of you who are reading for the first time, thank you for choosing this book. I'm looking forward to the success of the entire State Street Series; a collection of contemporary romance companion novels set in Madison, Wisconsin, my hometown. The books in this series revolve around the shops of State Street, Madison's renowned pedestrian mall, a place near and dear to my heart. My hope is to bring a little taste of State Street to each book through my storytelling while creating rich characters, exploring relationships and the little reasons people fall in love.

*I am always active on my social media accounts and I love connecting with my readers! You can visit my website at www.kristenmorgen.com and check out the following links for updates, cover reveals, new release dates, book reviews, book recommendations and more!*

Amazon: Kristen Morgen

Facebook Account: Kristen Morgen

Facebook Page: Kristen Morgen Author

Facebook Group: Kristen Morgen Beyond the

Book

Twitter: @kristenmorgen

Instagram: @kristen.morgen

Goodreads: Kristen Morgen

AllAuthor: Kristen Morgen

BookBub: Kristen Morgen

Email: kristen@kristenmorgen.com

# DEDICATION

*For my daughters, Sydney and Lindsey, the other little writers in my house.*

*Never stop writing, never stop imagining, and never lose sight of your dreams.*

# Acknowledgements

To Jason, for supporting me every step of the way, for encouraging me when I needed it, and for giving me the space I needed to spend endless hours doing my favourite thing in the world.

To my parents, for your unconditional love and support always, for being my first audience for this book, and for being the best listeners ever. Dad, you were my first writing coach and taught me more than you can imagine about being a good writer.

To Brandi, for being the most excited, enthusiastic, and supportive sister ever; every step of the way. I appreciate your encouragement more than you know.

To my family and friends, those of you who actually knew I was writing this book, thank you for cheering me on and making me feel so proud to be doing something I truly love. Jen, thanks for being my test audience and for giving me so much confidence in my work as a writer.

To my first editor, Margie Aston, for setting the bar high and being the awesome perfectionist that you are. My work is better for it. You really made this experience an enjoyable one.

To my readers, thank you for your reviews, your constant encouragement, your kind words and your unyielding support. It means the world to me. You have made this book a success and you have been the driving force to keep me going as a writer.

To Kemone and Tamarind Hill Press, thank you for welcoming me into your house and supporting my book and my vision as an author. You have made this process a wonderful one.

This book was years in the making and, at times, quite daunting to imagine actually finishing. I'm proud to say that the words of my late father-in-law, John, were always in the back of my mind while writing this book – *How do you eat an elephant? One bite at a time.*

# Table of Contents

**COMING SOON**

# Prologue

Darkness. Rebecca had never been afraid of it. Not because she was fearless, but because she understood that darkness was simply the absence of light.

She was intimately familiar with the delicate balance that existed between the dark and the light and embraced it. Exploring that balance in the world around her was as natural as breathing. Searching for it in everything, she had observed the contrast between the two for as long as she could remember.

That's what artists do. They see the world a little differently. While most people are simply looking at their environment, artists are *seeing* it. In an artist's mind, there are no limits to what will serve as inspiration. To a photographer, anything, from a single flower floating on a sweeping landscape to a couple sitting on a park bench, can be the next subject of study. Every subject has both light and dark; contrast and beauty.

Tonight, the darkness was comforting to her, as it usually was when she was in her darkroom. Other than the faint red glow of the safelight in the corner, it was like a starless night. She loved it and felt cradled by the tiny dark space that she called home. It was her safe zone, her creative oasis where she could delve into her art without interruption.

The darkroom wasn't much to look at, but it housed everything she needed to develop her black and white photographs. A small sink in the corner was flanked by counters on either side. An enlarger sat to one side of the sink, while shallow bins with various developing solutions sat on the other. Drying lines with photo clips hung in every direction along the only bare wall. Every possible cubic inch of the small room was used for storage of developing supplies and it felt more like a large closet than a room. But it got the job done.

Her darkroom ritual of developing photos had a rhythm to it, akin to a dance. She had established a method over the years, getting the exposure and contrast exactly how she wanted it. Developing prints from negatives in this manner gave her complete control and flexibility. Controlling that contrast between the dark and the light was her specialty, it was her gift.

She was forever in her comfort zone in her darkroom and usually had a good groove going. She always had her music playing in the background, which varied depending on her mood, and she was meticulously organized with her process. This familiar routine and rhythm always brought her peace.

On any other typical day, she would be developing a roll of film from a photo shoot she had just finished, but today was different. Today she was uncovering a mystery. She had found an old roll of

# Behind the Glass

film in a drawer at her mom's house last week and the curiosity was eating at her.

That's the thing with 'old fashioned' 35mm film. There is no record of what photos are contained within that tiny metal case and they are not date stamped. It was literally anyone's guess as to what was in there or when they were taken. Her mother was no help; she didn't even know the roll was in the drawer until Rebecca found it.

This roll of film could contain anything; from a photographic study she'd done for a local photography class to a private photo shoot she'd done for a friend. It could even be a series of random landscapes from the road trips she'd taken as a teen. She'd had that camera in her hand for as long as she could remember. It was part of who she was, and an extension of how she viewed the world.

Finding an undeveloped roll of film was exciting but not entirely surprising considering the hundreds of rolls she'd shot in her life. She chose to look at this as a gift; something to unwrap. Whatever was on this roll, she opted to reveal each photo one at a time, without looking at the negatives, just for fun. Each photo would serve as a little clue, leading her to when and where they were taken.

Inserting the first negative into the negative carrier at the top of the enlarger, she slowly adjusted the focus until the image was crystal clear. After adjusting the filters and f-stop settings, she placed a piece of photographic paper in the photo easel below. Setting the timer for six seconds, she pushed the timer button, exposing the paper to the light of the negative image, imprinting it onto the photographic paper.

With her curiosity building as to what the photo was of, she placed the photographic paper into the developer solution and waited for the image to emerge. She could only make out an image of a house from the negative, but it didn't look familiar to her. Slowly, as the developer solution did its job, the photo began to appear on the white paper like magic. A picture of her house on Beacon Street, the house she grew up in, could be seen as she tipped the tray back and forth, mixing the developer solution over the photo.

It was just a basic landscape with the house in the distance, slightly out of focus in areas, with an odd angle, but it was without a doubt the house she remembered from her childhood. The trees were still small, which indicated that the photo was from many years ago. She hadn't lived there since middle school, so these photos must have been taken when she was just starting out as a photographer. Smiling, she eagerly ran the photo through the stop bath, fixer and rinse baths before hanging it on the drying line and moving on to the next photo in the roll.

She spent the next hour unwrapping each new gift. Photos of her family dog, Rex, and her cat, Sam, took up a great deal of the film roll. Flowers, swing sets, her Husky ten-speed bike, friendship bracelets and various other inanimate objects gradually appeared on each piece of photographic paper. None indicated when the photos were taken or how old she was at the time. And with as many photos as she'd taken in her life, it was really anyone's guess.

Finally, a clue appeared. A picture of her younger brother, Trey, at age six or seven, which would make her... nine or ten, maybe? It wasn't the best photo of him, but hopefully there were more. Charged with excitement and now feeling like a full-fledged detective, she methodically stayed in her groove of developing each negative, photo by photo, revealing several more pictures of her brother and a few of one of her childhood girlfriends in their secret clubhouse.

Based on the photos, she speculated that she was close to ten years old when these were taken. The inexperience was obvious to her trained eye and it was probably one of the first rolls of film she'd ever taken. That would explain why she had almost no recollection of taking them. She didn't know it then, but these photographs, this childhood photo shoot, was the beginning of her future career and constant preoccupation with photography.

As she surveyed the photos hung all over her tiny darkroom, her memories began to slowly come into focus. Flashes of her childhood came in rushes. Her home on Beacon Street, her dog, her cat, her brother, her friends, they all felt less like distant memories as she studied the photos. There were so many...

The mystery film roll was almost finished, and each unwrapped gift had been a pleasant surprise. She had developed almost all the negatives now, all but one.

That last one was a surprise; one she wasn't expecting.

As the image slowly appeared on the photo paper, she was overwhelmed with emotion. Her heart pounded as she transferred it from tray to tray. She could feel the tears welling up as she hung the final photo on the drying line, taking a step back to admire it.

There was so much to process, so many emotions to sort through.

The photo itself was amateur at best. It was over-exposed in some areas, under-exposed in others, but the subject matter was what grabbed her attention. A young couple sat in a porch swing together, in a loving embrace, the woman's legs draped over the man's lap, the man's arm wrapped around the woman, both looking into each other's eyes with so much love. They were in their own little world, paying no attention to anything but each other.

It was a picture of her parents; a memory that was as clear to her now as yesterday. She knew in an instant how old she was when all these photos were taken. She was ten years old and this was the last summer they spent as a family of four. The last summer they were happy and carefree. Before the divorce.

# Behind the Glass

Sometimes she wished she could go back in time and be that girl again. To be that carefree ten-year-old girl who wanted nothing more than to take pictures of her dog and her friends and flowers. She longed for the innocence of childhood, before everything came tumbling down. But she wasn't that little girl anymore and would never be again.

Yes, she understood darkness. And despite everything she still wasn't afraid of it.

# CHAPTER ONE

*Rebecca*

Few people came here this late at night. The occasional patrons who did wander in at this hour were usually either weary college students needing a quick shot of espresso to keep going, flocks of lively young girls taking a short break before the second round of club-hopping, or on occasion, two lovers engaging in a secret romantic rendezvous.

During her many nights of coming here, she had seen it all.

It was just minutes to midnight, that wondrous part of the day when she finally allowed herself to slow down but wasn't quite ready for sleep just yet. She had grown to love this special part of the night that belonged only to her. It was undoubtedly her favourite time to come here.

After a long, arduous week, the serene calm and quiet solitude of her beloved bookstore café had become her most vital oasis. She had come here every week for months, always alone, always at this time of night, and she'd grown to love this stylish little shop's atmosphere. Something innocuous about it made her feel at home and she was completely at peace here. Her favourite soft velvet reading chair on the second floor could always be depended upon to be waiting for her.

The shop was an eclectic little gem tucked away inconspicuously into the fabric of downtown Madison, Wisconsin, on State Street, the city's renowned pedestrian mall. Set back slightly between the adjacent storefronts, its unadorned façade and soft lighting from within made it virtually glow from the street at night.

The open two-story space inside could be seen clearly from the street through a simple storefront consisting of virtually seamless glass. Its clean design contrasted sharply with the adjacent brick and stone facades, giving it a light, airy feel. The openness of its design was initially what drew her here. The shop itself was quite figuratively an open book.

Inside the shop, on either side of the entrance, three evenly-spaced, colourful glass light fixtures highlighted local artwork that the shop showcased to the public. Farther inside, the first floor's main space was filled with groupings of wood tables and chairs, large lush reading chairs, and oblong coffee tables displaying books.

Immense mahogany bookcases flanked each side of the main space and a simple granite café counter in the rear ran the entire width of the shop. A long staircase nestled into one side of the shop led to a loft area above that overlooked most of the main space below.

Unlike the first floor, the loft area above was a smaller, much more intimate space with quiet acoustics and soft lighting that made for an excellent reading environment. The gorgeous mahogany floors and dark textures in the cherry wood furniture brought warmth to the space, while the lighter wall colours and simple lines of the railings made it feel open and welcoming.

She made an immediate connection to this secluded area of the shop and habitually took refuge here each week, happily losing herself in her books and letting the busy world fall away for a while.

It was quiet at this late hour, other than the faint echo of a distant conversation and the soft music playing over the sound system. The acoustics throughout the shop were superb and the music set a relaxing tone. The inviting smells of rich coffee and baked goods filled virtually every cubic inch of the two-story space.

To her, it was heavenly, and she considered her nights here a true indulgence.

By nature, she had never been the type who took time like this for herself. She was focused, disciplined, and her daily obligations to her two jobs during the week took most of her time and energy. She was, by her definition, a struggling artist paying her dues and was willing to make the needed sacrifices.

By day, she worked as a staff photographer for the *Isthmus,* a local weekly newspaper in town. It wasn't a glamorous position by any stretch of the imagination, but it gave her a chance to do what she loved; photography was her passion. Intrigued by it since high school when she took an introductory class for her art elective Rebecca was immediately hooked. She had a natural eye for it and loved spending endless hours in the darkroom.

Her position didn't pay much, and the subject matter was usually somewhat menial, but she learned from it every day and expanded her education constantly. She captured the best of whatever assignment she was given on film, whether it was Madison's annual Art Fair on the Square or simply the pet of the week. Whatever the challenge, she was simply content to have her dependable, manual 35mm camera in hand.

The income from her daily job scarcely paid her bills, which made her second job an inevitable necessity. By night she worked as a waitress at a local high-end restaurant downtown, owned by a childhood friend's family. The hours were long and being on her feet all day was sometimes exhausting, but she couldn't deny how lucky she was to work there. The tips were lucrative and she truly couldn't ask for better people to work for.

It was actually while walking downtown after a long day of work one night that she discovered this wonderful little shop. The fact that the shop displayed local artwork every month was an added bonus. Inspired by it each week, she imagined seeing her photography in its windows one day.

Her weekly routine of escaping to this oasis over the past several months had become something Rebecca truly looked forward to. After the typical monotony of a long work week, she enjoyed treating herself to a caramel latte with whipped cream served in a large hand-thrown pottery mug. After exchanging pleasantries with the owners, she would always take her time to admire the local artwork as she walked upstairs to the loft area, and then quietly settled into her favourite comfy reading chair, eagerly getting lost in whatever book she was reading that week.

Her minutes-to-midnight ritual had become a comforting constant in her life.

This week as she walked upstairs to the loft with coffee in hand, something profoundly beautiful caught her eye in the artwork on the wall by the landing of the stairs. Tonight, one minor element of her evening routine was noticeably altered.

The local art normally displayed on the café walls each month was amateur at best. It was quite appealing to the untrained eye but was by no means extraordinary. The work of art before her tonight, however, was a striking exception.

As she halted on the landing, fascinated by the painting in front of her, her surroundings gradually faded away as she examined the work. It was unexplainable, but something about it captivated her deeply and the effect was magnetic. She was inescapably drawn to it.

The painting itself was no larger than a standard piece of paper, yet it appeared far more substantial to her. Framed in a simple white mat inside a basic black frame, the contrast in colours appeared sharp, yet soft simultaneously. In the foreground stood three abstract white houses set against a harsh black sky. A single blurry white line above indicated a distant skyline with dark looming blue-grey clouds above.

It wasn't the subject matter that caught her attention but rather the feeling the scene evoked. The landscape was mysteriously barren and cold, yet strangely welcoming. As her eyes carefully scanned every minute detail of the painting, she found herself wondering what it would feel like to be inside this peculiar space. She imagined it would probably feel cool, but not cold. The wind might be blowing softly, the way it does before a storm. It would likely be quiet and peaceful. Voices and sounds, if there even were any, might echo.

Then it hit her. The feeling she connected with so strongly was *loneliness.*

As if created only for her, this brilliant artist had captured the feeling of being completely alone in such a beautiful way. Her usual feeling of peace and contentment in this place became abruptly emotional as she realized why this painting spoke to her so completely.

Entirely lost in her own unsettling thoughts, the sharp sound of several ceramic coffee mugs crashing to the floor at once pulled her abruptly back to reality. She spun around quickly in surprise, momentarily losing her balance on the landing and almost spilling her hot coffee. Her heart jumped to her throat and she stopped breathing for a moment. She hadn't realized how detached she had become and nearly couldn't remember where she was.

It was then, as she quickly scanned the main space below her, immediately identifying the source of the startling clamour, that her eyes unexpectedly noticed *him*.

He was sitting alone at a table near the rear of the shop, staring directly up at her with stunningly intense eyes. It was his atypical expression that caught her eye; he looked as if he had been staring at her for a long while.

He was a genuinely handsome young man with soulful, deep-set dark brown eyes. His face was striking with flawless bone structure and a strong, square jaw. His short, dark brown hair was slightly tousled and he wore two-day-old scruff on his perfectly sculpted face. His lean build and broad shoulders were indicative of someone active and athletic. Dressed casually in jeans and a dark grey button-down shirt, he was, by all appearances, definitely a man women noticed when he walked into a room.

# Behind the Glass

He made absolutely no effort to look away and their eyes locked onto each other for a long moment. Feeling unexpectedly self-conscious, she could feel her face begin to flush and her heart begin to race. She wasn't used to being noticed this way by someone who looked the way he did. The intensity in his eyes continued but a slight look of curiosity began to emerge as his expression softened slightly.

Noticing this, she unconsciously tilted her head slightly and fought back a sudden urge to smile. Reluctantly, she finally forced herself to look away slowly, released from his intense gaze.

Flustered, she swiftly turned and headed upstairs, stumbling on the first step and not noticing what she dropped on the stair below. As she reached the top of the stairs she quickly made her way to her usual reading chair and settled in quietly, her heart still racing.

Unaware that a tiny smile had emerged on her lips, she felt goose bumps up and down her arms and nervous butterflies in her stomach. Rebecca had no idea who he was or why he had been staring at her so intently, but her curiosity and wonder made it nearly impossible to focus on her book or anything else.

A sudden shiver went down her back.

She focused and tried to think, trying to remember if he had been sitting there when she first walked in and ordered her coffee. Surely she would have noticed him, so it's possible he came in later. She wondered how long she had been admiring the painting but couldn't be sure. Maybe that was why he had been staring at her. She simply couldn't make sense of it.

Why would *he* notice *her*? She shook her head, smiling. It was definitely a mystery.

Ultimately deciding to shrug it off as nothing more than an isolated incident that would likely be forgotten by tomorrow, she tried not to give it any more thought and began refocusing on her evening. She was four chapters into her latest book and it was getting interesting, so diving back into it would be an excellent way to redirect her mind. The new author she was reading had a remarkable way of taking her far from reality, which was exactly what she needed tonight.

She took a few sips of her coffee and nestled comfortably into her chair.

Halfway through chapter five, she heard a faint creak at the top of the stairs. Quickly snapping her head up, she was completely stunned by what she saw. The handsome young man from downstairs was standing at the top step gazing in her direction clear across the second floor.

As she looked at him, her heart jumped and she silently caught her breath. An equal mix of excitement and panic shot through her as he started walking directly toward her, his beautiful eyes locked onto hers again.

He stopped squarely in front of her and handed her a familiar object.

# Behind the Glass

As she peered up at him, he seemed much taller than she had imagined and unbelievably, more handsome. His kind smirk and single raised eyebrow drew her in immediately.

"You dropped this on the stairs."

His voice was quite possibly the most mesmerizing she had ever heard.

Her heart pounded as every muscle in her body tensed up.

Rebecca struggled to release herself from his beautiful eyes to slowly look down at his outreached hand. The object he held was a beaded bookmark her mother had made for her on her last birthday. She obviously hadn't noticed she'd dropped it.

She took it from him slowly without a word, desperately trying to form a coherent thought. After a few moments a nearly inaudible '*thank you*' was all she could manage.

The way he looked at her and the way it made her feel seemed to prevent her from thinking clearly or acting normally. She continued to look at him, speechless.

He slowly sat down in the chair next to her with a subtle smile on his face.

"Are you alright?" he asked quietly.

There was something so familiar about his voice, as if she'd known him for a long time. She couldn't understand it but his tone seemed to instantly put her at ease.

"I'm fine," she answered as calmly as possible. "Why?"

She could only imagine what she must look like from his perspective. She wasn't normally this tongue-tied and she hoped he didn't think there was something wrong with her.

"You look like your mind is somewhere else right now, somewhere far away."

He was perceptive. Her mind *was* somewhere else. And completely blank.

"Yes," she began, desperately trying to focus. "I suppose it is. I... I usually come here to relax. It must be working."

Wondering if she had even made sense, it was the best she could come up with for now. As her heart rate finally approached normal, she slowly started to relax a little.

"So that's why you come here then," he asked with a raised eyebrow, "to relax?"

She wondered about the suspicious tone in his voice.

"Yes, this shop is a great place to unwind."

"Interesting."

Again, his tone made her wonder.

"Why is that interesting?" she tried to read his eyes.

His expression had changed as if he knew something she didn't.

"You look like you come here to hide."

His eyes met hers again as he spoke, carefully watching her reaction.

To her surprise his comment hit a nerve and her mind began to race. She came here to *hide*? She couldn't imagine what possible interest he would have in her reasons for coming here and wondered why he would say something like that to someone he didn't know.

"And what would I be hiding from exactly?"

"You tell me."

His stunning eyes studied her reaction again as if he knew what she was thinking.

"I'm not hiding from anything," she asserted, her tone slightly more defensive than intended. She tried to understand where this conversation was leading.

He shook his head and smiled. His breath-taking smile practically knocked her over. It was the most beautiful thing she had ever seen in her life. He definitely had an unfair advantage looking the way he did, and she was finding it hard to keep her focus.

"Sure," he speculated, "you come here to *relax*."

"Why is that so hard to believe?" She was truly intrigued.

"So," he began thoughtfully, "you choose this hour at night, when the shop is practically empty, to come and sip coffee and read a book, something you could easily do at home. You didn't come with anyone and I'm guessing no one even knows you're here. If you're not hiding from anything, then why not stay at home and read?"

Tilting her head slightly, she glared at him, unsure what to make of what he had just said. She wondered how he had even known about her weekly routine. Had he been here before?

She felt the blood rush to her face.

"I honestly don't see how this is any of your business, but I happen to like this place. It's... tranquil. And I love coming here. It's actually a great little shop with a lot to offer."

She knew she was reaching but it seemed to make sense.

"You come here for the artwork," he stated with a subtle sarcastic tone.

Again his comment hit another nerve.

"The artwork happens to be exceptional this month. I'll admit it's not always at a particularly high level but it's encouraging to see people putting themselves out there like that. It's inspirational." *Maybe one day, if I dare to be brave enough, my photography will be displayed here too*, she thought to herself.

"This month?"

"Excuse me?"

"You said the artwork is exceptional *this month*," he clarified. His expression was suddenly warm again. She looked into his deep brown eyes, instantly shaking off their previous conversation and recalled the beautiful painting at the stairs' landing.

"Yes," she began thoughtfully, "it's wonderful." She paused for a moment, remembering how the painting had affected her so deeply. "The artist this month is extremely talented. There's a depth to the work that's very raw."

He took a moment before responding.

"You seem to appreciate art. To really connect to it, I mean. That's a rare thing. You seemed to really like the painting by the stairs earlier."

Embarrassed, she realized he must have been watching her when she was admiring it for what she assumed to be a noticeably long time.

"Yes, I guess you noticed that."

"It was hard not to," he replied, smiling warmly.

His stunning smile made her heart skip a beat. She returned the smile involuntarily.

"I was *connecting,* as you put it."

Feeling slightly uncomfortable, she hoped he would change the subject.

"What did you like about it?"

His curiosity was puzzling. She couldn't understand why this ridiculously attractive stranger she had just met had so many questions for her. When she looked at him he appeared genuinely interested in her answer.

"I generally don't connect with art unless I can relate to something I see in it. The painting by the stairs..." She paused, carefully choosing her words. "I could imagine being in that scene, what the physical environment would feel like to me, how being there would make me feel, what the artist may have been trying to convey. If it touches me on an emotional level, I like it. For me, that's what art is supposed to do. Of course it's different for everyone."

He quietly focused on her, listening intently, hanging onto her every word without responding. He looked somewhat reflective, taking in what she just said. She felt slightly self-conscious, hoping she made sense. She tended to ramble when she discussed art.

Taking a sip of her now lukewarm coffee, she decided to try to change the course of the conversation. Rebecca had been cooperative thus far and had answered his questions. In fact, she had been more truthful than she had intended. Something about him made her feel less guarded and her words seemed to pour out, unfiltered.

This handsome stranger was surprisingly easy to talk to.

"So, why do *you* come here at this hour? Is it the artwork or do you just enjoy interrogating strangers?" She tried to keep her tone light so he knew she was joking. He smiled, obviously enjoying her sense of humour.

"I know the owners. They're old friends of mine. And for the record, I wasn't interrogating you. I apologize if that's how I came across." He sounded sincere. "You just intrigue me."

She *intrigued* him?

Apparently he had more of an interest in her than she originally thought. As she considered this, she slowly began to realize that this may not have been the first night they had been there together. If he knew the owners then surely he would know how often she came there and when. Over the many months she'd been visiting the shop, the husband and wife owners began to anticipate her weekly arrival. But why would they tell him about one of their customers? The more she pondered the idea, the crazier it sounded.

"Why is that exactly?" she asked, trying to read his eyes.

He hesitated slightly before he answered.

"Let's just say you're a bit of a mystery to me, an unsolved puzzle."

Now that was ironic. *She* was the mystery here?

"So it's puzzling to you that I come to a bookstore café late at night and like to read alone? Some people just like their *me time*. How is that unusual?"

"It's not. But that's not why you come here," he clarified, with the same intense expression he had downstairs.

The finality of his tone made her feel as if he knew much more about her than he was letting on, and ultimately made her realize something that she hadn't wanted to admit to herself. He was right on target.

"That's not the only mystery," he added before she had a chance to respond.

Implying more than she thought he intended, she was given a perfect opportunity and her curiosity couldn't let it go.

"So, how can I be so intriguing to you in such a short period of time? We just met. You don't know anything about me."

He looked down and paused momentarily before answering.

"Tonight... isn't the first time I've seen you here," he admitted, still looking down. "I've been here late at night before." He slowly looked up at her, carefully reading her expression.

As it finally started making sense, she was filled with an unexpected flood of emotions. She was both flattered and profoundly confused at his interest in her. Realizing that he had likely been watching her for who knows how long actually didn't make her feel uncomfortable, which surprised her. If anything, his very presence put her at ease.

"How long?" she asked softly. It was all she could manage to say. His piercing gaze made it hard to concentrate again.

He seemed to know exactly what she was asking.

"A while," he said quietly, "longer than I'd like to admit."

Her heart skipped a beat and a chill went down her back. He noticed her reaction and smiled apologetically. She didn't quite know what to make of all of this but strangely, was far from being upset by it.

"Did you know I'd be here tonight?"

"Yes," he replied evenly.

# Behind the Glass

She wondered how many nights she had come here in the last several weeks when he had been here too. She never *really* took notice of the other customers in the shop, but surely she would have noticed *him*. She wondered how lost in her books she usually got when she was here. Would she have even been aware of a secret admirer, if that's what he was? It sounded absurd.

"Why did you choose tonight to talk to me?"

"That wasn't entirely planned. You saw me downstairs."

It was hard not to. His presence was simply magnetic, drawing her in as he observed her from afar. She almost blushed again as she remembered.

"But you came upstairs, to me."

He held up the bookmark and smiled.

"You gave me an excuse."

She couldn't get used to his smile. It was overwhelming. She tried in vain to get a hold of herself. It wasn't just his beauty that made her feel the way she did. When he looked at her and spoke to her this way she felt connected to him in a genuinely real way. It was unfamiliar and as much as she didn't want to admit it, wonderful.

He sensed her apparent uneasiness and leaned away from her slightly in an attempt to put her at ease.

"I apologize if this is strange for you. I didn't mean to make you uncomfortable."

The words *strange* or *uncomfortable* didn't seem to apply here. Truthfully she couldn't find a word for what she felt at this moment.

"Strange no, confusing maybe."

This threw him completely.

"Why is it *confusing*?"

She didn't exactly know how to explain it to him or even to herself. This whole scenario was definitely unchartered territory for her.

"It's just hard for me to understand... why *you* would take so much of an interest in *me*." *Or even notice me for that matter,* she thought to herself.

His expression was hard, unreadable for a few moments, until it finally softened as if he had just solved a puzzle. He smiled softly and looked directly into her eyes as he leaned in again.

"Trust me, from *my* perspective it's *extremely* easy to understand."

He didn't elaborate. He simply looked at her with warm eyes as if trying to convey the extent of his feelings. His answer was somewhat cryptic yet she knew exactly what he meant. For some unfathomable reason he was drawn to her. To say that she was drawn to him as well was an understatement. The attraction was instant and magnetic.

As she leaned in slightly looking into his eyes, she realized his answer pleased her more than she wanted to admit. It was hard to believe she could have feelings of this magnitude toward someone she had just met and it didn't make sense to her.

# Behind the Glass

Things like this didn't happen every day, she knew that, and not to her, yet she wished she could understand why tonight of all nights their paths had crossed.

As the reality of the situation began to finally settle in, anxiety inevitably shot through her and a sinking feeling in the pit of her stomach told her she should probably go home. As difficult as it was, her instincts told her that leaving was the right thing to do.

Looking away from him she subtly began gathering her things.

Oblivious to her sudden internal battle he interrupted her before she could leave.

"I have another question, if you don't mind," he asked politely.

She knew she shouldn't stay any longer, but she was curious.

"Imagine that," she replied with a smile, trying to stay casual.

He returned the smile, sensing her apprehension.

"Earlier you said that if art touches you on an emotional level, you like it. I was wondering how the painting made you feel."

He seemed to have an uncanny ability to ask the one question she had no desire to answer. She couldn't imagine why it mattered to him what she thought of the painting, and tried to think of a way to answer him without admitting too much.

"It's hard to put it into words," she shrugged her shoulders. "Art is a personal thing."

As she looked down she realized it was difficult to be anything but completely honest when she looked at him and she didn't trust herself.

His silence told her he respected her privacy, which she appreciated.

As they sat quietly together in a comfortable silence, she reflected on how incredibly rare this whole thing was. This was definitely not how she had envisioned her evening playing out tonight, meeting *him*.

Though her heart was telling her to stay there with him, her rational, determined mind was stronger, as always. She had answered his final question and it was now time to go.

Slowly she gathered her things and stood up. He looked up at her, clearly trying to understand what was happening. She stood in place for a moment not wanting to move. She could feel his eyes on her as she took a small step forward.

"Don't go," he whispered.

Her heart sank. She took another small step.

"Please," he said, slightly louder.

She stopped and was now standing next to him, only inches away.

Deep down she wanted to stay, she couldn't deny that. Rebecca wanted to learn everything there was to know about this man, wanted to answer any question he asked, wanted to talk to him for hours. But she had to leave. She had her own reasons for leaving and she wished she could explain them to him.

"I think I should go now," she barely uttered, taking another step.

"Wait," he said, looking up at her. "You said that I don't know you, or anything about you."

"Yes."

She didn't look at him, afraid of what she might do or say if she did.

"I'd like to, very much."

In a flash, she was sure that every ounce of blood in her body had reached her face at once and she instantly felt hot. She felt light headed and her heart began to race again. She could feel his eyes on her and desperately wanted to look at him.

She tried to focus and think of what to say.

"I'm flattered," she breathed, "but I can't. I'm sorry, I wish I could." More than he would ever know she wished she could stay there with him. "I really have to go."

As she took a few more steps, he stood up. He appeared as if he was about to follow her but something stopped him. In response she halted, as if being pulled back toward him.

He stood in place for a moment before slowly walking toward her. He lightly touched her hand with his as she quickly looked up at him. His light touch was unexpectedly amazing. Every nerve in her body suddenly seemed to come alive at once. It was the first time they had stood face-to-face and she noticed that he was a good bit taller than she was. His broad stance dominated the space, unintentionally pulling her toward him. Her heart felt as if it would pound out of her chest as she looked up into his stunning eyes.

"Will you please give me one thing then?"

At this moment she would have given him anything he asked for.

"Yes," her voice cracked into a whisper.

"Your name."

Surprised by his simple request, she breathed a sigh of relief. She didn't know if she would ever see him again and if nothing else, she was actually comforted by the idea of him knowing her name.

"Rebecca," she answered evenly, looking into his soulful brown eyes one last time.

As a faint smile crossed her face she slowly looked away and started toward the stairs, feeling his eyes on her with every step.

She hesitated for a moment at the top step, wanting to look back at him again but thought better of it. The temptation to stay would be too much to resist.

Closing her eyes, she took a deep breath, trying to ignore the sinking feeling overtaking her. Before she could change her mind, she quickly opened her eyes and pushed forward, down the stairs and out the front door of her wonderful oasis without looking back.

# CHAPTER TWO

*Michael*

Recalling every detail of her face, her smile, her voice, her delicate figure, had gradually become an addiction. Utterly preoccupied with a longing he'd never experienced before, he thought about her every single day.

Two weeks had passed since meeting her at the bookstore café. He simply couldn't get the beautiful image of Rebecca out of his mind. After only one short meeting he had every line of her face completely memorized.

Simply put, she was the most classical beauty he had ever seen.

She didn't wear much makeup, only a hint of it on her lips and long eyelashes. Her perfect face didn't need makeup; her beauty was natural and effortless. Her long, flowing, light bronze hair surrounded the soft jawline of an angelic face with flawless ivory skin. Her slightly full lips enhanced her breath-taking smile and her thin high eyebrows framed the most gorgeous deep green eyes ever created. Initially he hadn't taken notice of her stunning eyes, but soon after meeting her face-to-face, they quickly became his favourite feature.

A week earlier he had hoped to see her again. Being the creature of habit she seemed to be, he knew he could depend on her weekly ritual. He arrived at the bookstore early, filled with anticipation and waited for her all night.

Ultimately to his disappointment, she did not come.

He recalled their conversation in his mind, repeatedly trying to understand what had gone wrong. He wondered if he had been too inquisitive and straightforward. He hoped he hadn't offended her when he guessed correctly as to why she came there. He found it impossible to be anything but completely honest when he looked into her emerald eyes, and he hoped his honesty hadn't driven her away.

Despite his confusion he was absolutely sure of one thing – he *knew* there was a connection between them. He wasn't imagining it and he knew she had felt it too. It was unlike anything he had ever experienced before. Their attraction was magnetic, natural, and immediate. He couldn't understand why she had left so abruptly.

He hadn't planned on talking to her that night. After weeks of building up the nerve to approach her, he couldn't waste the opportunity the bookmark she had dropped on the stairs presented him. It was an irresistible temptation and the perfect excuse to go to her.

He simply couldn't stay away from her any longer.

# Behind the Glass

She was unique, impossible not to notice. An endless puzzle, completely fascinating, he wanted nothing more than to learn more about her.

For weeks she had been coming to the bookstore café at exactly the same time each Friday night, ordering her usual latte, discretely retreating upstairs and reading until closing time.

And she was *always* alone.

One would think that a beautiful young girl such as Rebecca would typically be out with friends or even a boyfriend on a Friday night. Instead she chose to hide away and escape into her books – on schedule, like clockwork.

Unnoticed by most, she also seemed to have a subtle sadness in her eyes which only kindled his interest in her further. It actually drew him to her. More than anything he wanted to know why. What was she hiding from?

He presumed it was only coincidence that she didn't come to the shop last week. Knowing only her first name, returning to the shop where they had first met was the only way he hoped to see her again. Determined to find her, he would wait for her again tonight.

On this particular Friday evening, the hours seem to pass by at an annoyingly slow pace and the anticipation of tonight's possible meeting with her was slowly consuming his thoughts.

Fortunately he had made plans tonight that would serve as a welcome distraction.

Under normal circumstances, a gathering at a local dance club downtown celebrating a friend's engagement would be the last place he would find himself, but tonight it would be a preferable way to pass the time.

In any case, he had gotten a good amount of grief from the guest of honour, a close college friend of his, about being practically antisocial these days. He had a strong feeling he wouldn't have been able to get out of it anyway.

His friend's name was Leo Prescott. They met in college during their first semester at the University of Wisconsin at Madison after discovering a shared loved of hiking and had been good friends since. Leo was probably one of the most genuine people Michael had ever met. He was loyal, with strong morals, and they clicked immediately for that reason. Leo was an open book and it was easy being friends with a person of his character.

He was a big guy, tall and muscular, and could look immensely intimidating at times. His personality, however, contrasted sharply with his appearance. He had a kind, gentle soul, almost childlike at times, with a remarkable sense of humour and an unmatched ability of bringing a room to life when he was in it.

His parents owned Azure, a restaurant in town that had started from nothing and over many years had become one of the most popular and exclusive in town. Leo had worked there most of his life and planned to take it over one day when his parents decided to retire. He took great pride in the family business and being his father's successor.

Leo was engaged to his long time love, Isabel Randolph. She was petite with blonde hair and blue eyes. Like Leo, she was kind-hearted and virtuous to the core. She was more of an introvert in comparison, quiet and shy. She cherished working with children and adored being a paediatric nurse at a local practice in town. They were completely enamoured with each other and had been together since their second year of college.

Leo popped the question months ago, immediately after graduation, but due to their busy schedules they hadn't officially celebrated the news with their friends until now. The wedding was only a little over a month away.

Although Michael and Leo had remained close friends throughout college they rarely saw each other anymore. The restaurant and Isabel took most of Leo's time and Michael had been unintentionally out of touch.

As much as he dreaded the coming evening, he was actually looking forward to seeing Leo again after so long. Seeing two people so deservingly happy together was inspirational and he was genuinely pleased for his friend.

He arrived at the dance club fashionably late. There was nothing worse than being the first poor soul to arrive with no one to talk to in a room full of adoring available women ready to proposition him.

The women at these dance clubs held little to no interest to him and were far from his type. They were usually either overly flirtatious, completely full of themselves, shallow, or more often than not, not much for intelligent conversation.

As a general rule he avoided places like these. For reasons he didn't always understand, he was frequently the object of desire for many of these club-hopping women, none of whom interested him in the least.

Michael had never been a fan of one-night stands or dating someone only a few times before moving on to the next 'conquest' like most of the male population at these dance clubs. He simply wasn't like that and never would be. When he met someone, he considered the future with her in the long-term, connecting with her on a deeper level, and spending time together. Simply put, he wanted *more*.

And now, only one person occupied his every thought.

He made his way through the immense, crowded upper level of the dance club, weaving his way through groupings of people at tall tables toward the main bar area overlooking the large dance floor below. Scanning the club for his friend, he took no notice of the dozens of women frozen in lustful awe as he walked by.

He quickly located Leo, his massive presence making him hard to miss, leaning next to a long metal railing separating the two levels of the club. Leo was talking to someone Michael recognized, another friend named Jared, who had sometimes joined them on their many hiking trips.

He couldn't recall Jared's last name but knew that he was one of Leo's many fraternity brothers back in college. He remembered Jared as being a somewhat shallow person which explained his obvious comfort level in a place like this.

He appeared to be vaguely listening to what Leo was saying but his eyes were constantly scanning the dance floor, trying to make eye contact with an equally eager young girl looking for a hook-up for the evening.

Leo stopped mid-conversation the moment he saw Michael.

"There he is!" Leo shouted, shaking hands and half hugging Michael. "I have to say, man, I had my doubts about seeing you here tonight. I'm glad you came!"

Feeling slightly guilty, Michael admitted, "Yeah, it's been a while. Sorry about that, man. It's good to see you."

"You, too. Where have you been hiding these days? I haven't seen or heard from you in months. What have you been up to?"

The term *hiding* certainly was ironic.

"Nothing much really, the usual," he said, determined to change the subject. "What about you? Where's your bride-to-be?"

Leo smiled proudly as his face instantly lit up. He glanced down toward the dance floor. Michael could see the affection in his eyes the instant his gaze met Isabel's.

"She's down there dancing with a couple friends," he said smiling, without taking his eyes off of her. He looked back to Michael and asked, "Hey, man, what can I get you to drink? I was just about to make a trip to the bar."

"A beer is fine, whatever you guys are drinking, thanks."

"Sure thing, be right back," Leo said, and quickly made his way toward the bar.

It was then, as Michael casually looked down toward the dance floor trying to spot Isabel that he saw something completely unexpected.

He thought at first that his eyes were deceiving him and that his imagination was running wild, but as his eyes focused through the glowing mass of dancers on the immense dance floor, amidst countless flashing lights, he was fairly certain he saw *her*.

Admittedly she was probably the last person he would expect to see in a dance club such as this and it didn't make sense to him that she would be here. Frankly, it seemed contradictory to everything he had observed about her.

# Behind the Glass

He focused again for a better look and for one crystal clear moment he could see the beautiful face he had been visualizing for the past two weeks. He had absolutely no doubt now – it was Rebecca.

As the music pounded and the lights flashed on her in varying colours, there was an indescribable aura surrounding her. She was dancing differently from every other girl on the dance floor. Her eyes were closed and she mouthed every word to the song playing. She responded uninhibitedly to the music, lost in her own world.

She was an amazing dancer and her dancing style was extremely sensual but not in a deliberate way. She paid no attention to anyone around her, and danced as if she was the only one on the dance floor. It also appeared that every male set of eyes was on her.

It was truly a side of her Michael had never expected.

The girl he saw dancing was drastically different from the one he knew from the bookstore café. She was free from anything she had been hiding from and the sadness was completely gone. It was as if the music had liberated her from these mundane worries along with any inhibitions she had. Amazingly, she was even more extraordinary than he had remembered.

She was nothing shy of perfect.

He couldn't deny the bizarre coincidence of the two of them being there tonight together but couldn't help being completely elated to finally see her again.

"Nice, right?" Jared asked, clearly amused.

Michael hadn't even realized he was still standing next to someone. He also hadn't been aware of his own reaction to seeing her dancing. He tried to snap himself out of the trance he was in, but it was difficult.

"What's that?"

He had no idea what Jared was referring to.

"Rebecca," Jared replied with a sleazy undertone.

Caught completely off guard, he couldn't be sure if Jared had just said her name or if he was imagining it.

"What did you just say?" Michael asked, trying not to sound too anxious.

"Rebecca," Jared clarified, "the girl dancing next to Isabel down there."

Michael looked again and now noticed that Rebecca and Isabel were dancing next to each other, something he obviously had failed to notice before.

Confused, he couldn't put it together.

"She's Brett's latest 'flavour of the month,'" Jared explained, smiling widely.

That couldn't be right. Michael must have heard him wrong.

"Brett and ... *Rebecca*?" he muttered, confused.

"Yeah, Leo set them up a few months ago. I guess Leo's known Rebecca forever. I think Brett must be going for a record or something. This is the longest he's been with anyone. Crazy, huh?"

Crazy didn't even scratch the surface.

*Brett Logan?* This made absolutely no sense to him. Michael didn't know Brett well, but what he did know wasn't entirely good. He was another of Leo's many fraternity brothers back in college and was, for lack of a better word, a player. He had a different girlfriend every weekend from what Michael remembered. He wasn't necessarily a bad guy; he just had a short attention span when it came to women.

Maybe he had changed. Maybe Rebecca had changed him. Michael could certainly understand how someone like Rebecca could turn anyone's world upside down. Regardless, he couldn't understand it. He knew little of her personality, but from what he did know, Brett Logan was quite possibly the *last* person he would have expected her to be with.

As he tried to make sense of it, his confusion was quickly being overshadowed by another strong emotion. As much as he tried to suppress his immediate jealousy, it was an exercise in futility.

It was completely illogical to feel threatened and he knew it. He didn't even know Rebecca and certainly didn't have the right to feel this way, but the connection he felt with her seemed to contradict all of that now. He could feel the adrenaline building.

"Where's Brett?" he asked casually. "I didn't see him anywhere."

"Oh, he'll be here later. He had something to take care of first."

Michael could only imagine what or whom Brett was taking care of.

As if Leo knew how badly Michael needed a distraction at that exact moment, he finally appeared with handfuls of drinks and an infectious smile on his face.

"This should get us started," he bellowed as he handed a beer to each of them. "So, what's up, people?" He smiled widely as if he was ready to get into some trouble.

"I was just telling Michael about Brett's girlfriend," Jared interjected.

The term *girlfriend* made Michael cringe internally.

"Oh yeah, Rebecca!" Leo responded, smiling. "I need to introduce you to her when they come back up. She's an awesome girl!"

She certainly was. And somehow, as fate would have it, Leo knew her and knew her well from the sound of it. As Michael tried to wrap his mind around the situation, his curiosity quickly started taking over.

"Jared said she's an old friend of yours?"

"Yeah, she is. She's more like the sister I never had actually. Our parents have been good friends for years, and I've known her since we were in diapers together, if you can imagine that. I can't believe I haven't mentioned her before."

# Behind the Glass

Neither could Michael. He was absolutely baffled at what a small world it was.

"She actually works as a waitress at Azure on week nights. You haven't been in for a while though, as I recall," he teased sarcastically.

Michael was grateful for another small, yet interesting insight into her daily life. Knowing where she could be found on a regular basis was actually comforting. The past two weeks had been difficult for him, not knowing anything about her except her first name. Not knowing if he would ever see her again.

"Yeah, it's been a while," Michael admitted. "I'll have to stop by sometime."

"You really should. It would be nice to see more of you."

As the music changed, Leo glanced down toward the dance floor and smiled widely.

"Here they come," he gestured to three figures making their way through the crowded dance floor toward the bar area.

A wave of thoughts and emotions ran through Michael's mind as he composed himself for the coming introduction. He had no idea what to expect. He wondered how Rebecca would react to seeing him again, and in this new situation.

His eyes searched through the glowing sea of people below until he finally saw the three of them several yards away. They were talking to one another and were moving slowly due to a bottleneck at the bottom of the stairs.

The wonderful carelessness he saw in Rebecca earlier on the dance floor was gone now and her expression was more melancholy. Again, Michael wondered why.

Rebecca and Isabel were with another girl he didn't recognize. She looked like a typical socialite who wore way too much makeup and not enough clothing. She had long, flowing bleached-blonde hair, a tall slender figure, and was as gorgeous as any runway model. And she knew it. She had an overconfidence about her that had most of the men in the room staring after her. She certainly had Jared's attention anyway.

As they made their way toward the table, Leo stepped forward and scooped Isabel up into his arms giving her a tight squeeze. She looked like a rag doll in his arms and appeared to be half his height. He gently placed her back down on the ground, gave her a tender kiss on the forehead, and stepped aside to let Rebecca by.

Rebecca gave Leo a relaxed, familiar smile as she passed him. The moment her eyes met Michael's, she came to an abrupt halt in sheer surprise.

Wide-eyed, she stared at Michael in disbelief, appearing as if she had stopped breathing. Michael couldn't help but smile, not at her apparent discomfort, but because of how instantly affected he was at seeing her again.

Leo gently took her by the arm.

# Behind the Glass

"I'd like to introduce you to a friend of mine from college. This is Michael."

Still frozen where she stood, she said nothing. She had the same blank expression on her face as the first time they met, but this time there was panic in her eyes.

Michael quickly speculated as to why and decided to let her off the hook.

He extended his hand to shake hers. "It's nice to meet you..." he trailed off, leaving her an opportunity to say her name.

She finally exhaled, "Rebecca."

She smiled apologetically with deep gratitude in her eyes as they shook hands. The moment their hands met, her gorgeous ivory skin flushed pink. Her soft touch was as heavenly as he had remembered. He returned the look as if to say, *you're welcome.*

"Rebecca," he repeated, smiling warmly.

It was clear that Rebecca had no intention of explaining their previous meeting and her silence confirmed that her Friday night hideout was, in fact, a secret.

They shook hands slightly longer than necessary, locking eyes until they were abruptly interrupted. The tall blonde had made her way past Leo, next to Rebecca, and extended her hand out to Michael.

"Hi, I'm Claire," she announced, flirtatiously.

Michael slowly took his eyes off Rebecca and politely shook Claire's hand.

"It's nice to meet you," he replied coolly.

He glanced back at Rebecca who subtly rolled her eyes. Michael smirked in response.

"So Michael, how do you and Leo know each other? I can't believe I haven't met you before," Claire flirted, trying to be charming.

Before Michael could answer, Leo interjected.

"Michael and I used to go hiking together a lot back in college. Didn't we meet during our first semester?"

"Yeah, English Lit, I think."

Michael clearly didn't enjoy being the center of attention at the moment.

"Right, English Lit! I wouldn't have passed that class without you, man. It wasn't exactly my subject, unlike *you*."

Michael glanced at Rebecca again, wondering what she must be thinking. He tried to read her expression, but she looked down soon after their eyes met, clearly as uncomfortable as he was.

"Mmmm... good-looking *and* smart," Claire purred, smiling widely at Michael as she squeezed his forearm.

Michael's uneasiness to Claire's amorous behaviour was obvious to everyone but Claire. Sensing this, Leo winked at him and as the music changed again he turned to Isabel.

"Alright girl, you owe me a dance! Let's go!"

Isabel smiled widely and enthusiastically grabbed his hand as they headed toward the stairs together. Claire began to follow them, hesitated, then swung her luscious blonde locks over her shoulder and glanced coyly back at Michael.

"Are you coming with us, Michael?" she asked in an overly seductive tone.

Michael tried to contain his distaste and answered as politely as possible, "No thanks, you go on ahead." He hoped she would concede.

"Alright," she pouted, turning at the stairs, "but I hope you'll change your mind." She shot a quick look toward Rebecca. "Are you coming, Bec?"

Rebecca glanced in Michael's direction for a moment.

"No, I think I'll sit this one out."

Michael tried to conceal a smile.

Jared practically bolted from his seat, smiling slyly at Michael, and caught up to Claire quickly. The four made their way down to the dance floor leaving Michael and Rebecca alone together.

Logically, Michael knew that at least a part of him should feel disappointed knowing that Rebecca was not available to him, knowing that Brett was the reason she had left that night, probably the reason she hadn't come back the following week, and the reason she wouldn't have come back later tonight, but he wasn't. He was just content to be with her again. He was pleasantly surprised that she chose to stay with him instead of going with her friends, grateful for any time he could have with her.

Her loyalty to Brett, no matter how misplaced he thought it may be, was actually a remarkably admirable trait. Oddly, it actually made her even more appealing to him. She had good morals.

Determined to make the best of their short time together, he pulled a chair out and gestured to her to sit down. She sat without a word, looking up at him with wide curious eyes.

As he sat across the table from her, he wondered what was going through her mind and assumed she probably had plenty of questions.

"So," he began, "it seems we have mutual friends."

Her anxious expression faded and her tense shoulders relaxed slightly.

"Yes, Leo seems to know everyone."

He sensed edginess in her voice and suspected it had something to do with Brett's impending arrival. He decided to keep things light and steer the conversation away from the subject of her boyfriend.

"I see you like to dance."

He smiled, remembering how stunning she had looked.

Her face instantly blushed red as she looked down at the table.

"Did you... see me dancing?" She was obviously self-conscious.

This confused him and he wondered why it would embarrass her.

"Yes. You're very... *different* when you dance. You looked amazing."

# Behind the Glass

He couldn't seem to find an adjective that could adequately describe what she had looked like out there. It was definitely an image that would stay with him for a long time.

She smiled and looked more at ease. His compliment had clearly pleased her.

"Thanks," she finally said. "How am I different though?"

He smiled immediately. Was she seriously *that* unaware of her effect on virtually every male within a fifty-foot radius on the dance floor? Clearly she didn't recognize how dramatically opposite from her bookstore café persona she was when she danced.

"You just looked truly happy, completely free from everything. The way you moved to the music... It was as if dancing let you escape."

She gently folded her arms and subtly avoided eye contact. Based on her reaction, it seemed he was right on target, again. As always, she was completely fascinating.

"I seem to have a knack for making you uncomfortable. I apologize."

She looked up and smiled, "No, you're right. That's exactly what happens when I'm out there. You just notice more about me than I'm used to, more than most people."

"It's hard not to," he replied, automatically. The words came out without thought and he instantly regretted saying them. As much as he wanted to tell her how he felt, he didn't want to make her more uncomfortable.

"Apparently," she said, shaking her head, in confusion. He could see that she still seemed completely baffled at his interest in her.

"Thank you, for earlier, by the way. I wasn't sure how to explain how I knew you."

Her cherished oasis was clearly something she chose to keep to herself.

"Your secret is safe with me."

"My secret?"

"Your bookstore café hideout."

"Oh," she sighed, "right, that."

He could see that she was clearly thinking of something else entirely, but had no clue as to what. He couldn't let it go.

"Do you have other secrets?"

"No," she hesitated, "just my *hideout,* as you put it."

She was withholding something, but he wasn't going to push it further.

Instead, he said something he couldn't seem to stop himself from saying.

"You didn't hide last week though." He locked eyes with her again.

Her expression instantly changed. She looked back at him with intense, tortured eyes. There was a long moment of silence between them and he could sense she was collecting her thoughts. The flashing lights and loud music of the dance club seemed to fade away slowly, and for a few moments as he looked at her it felt as if they were the only two people in the world.

"I wanted to come. More than anything. I just *couldn't.*" Her sad eyes spoke volumes.

Knowing the truth was more difficult than he could have ever anticipated.

She *did* want to be with him, he hadn't been imagining it. Their connection was real and it was the most incredible thing he had ever experienced with anyone.

But she belonged to someone else.

"Brett," he stated sombrely. There was nothing else he could say.

She frowned slightly at hearing his name out loud. For the first time the sadness in her eyes made sense to him.

"Brett," she echoed softly. "I'm *so* sorry."

It troubled him seeing her this way. A sudden unexpected need to hold her, to somehow comfort her, was overpowering. Steeling himself, he resolved to make things easier for her.

"You can go back to your bookstore. I promise not to bother you anymore."

She looked defeated, as if this was the last thing she wanted to hear.

"No, you don't bother me, really. The last thing you do is *bother* me. Actually, I really want..." she stopped mid-sentence and looked off in the distance behind him. A mix of panic and anguish filled her eyes. Michael knew immediately their time alone together was about to end. As much as he dreaded this moment, it was inevitable.

Brett appeared at Rebecca's side, greeted her, and gave her a quick familiar hug and a soft kiss on the cheek. She smiled automatically in response but the smile didn't reach her eyes. Her entire body seemed as rigid as stone. She looked back at Michael nervously, her face flush.

Brett turned toward Michael in genuine surprise. "Michael! Hey, man, I haven't seen you in ages! Leo said you might be here tonight. It's good to see you!" He shook Michael's hand.

Brett was a generically good-looking guy with a medium height and build. He had short blonde hair with a light complexion, and always appeared somewhat polished. Although he had stopped playing sports in college, his jock persona hadn't changed one bit. The only noticeable difference Michael could see was Rebecca's obvious effect on him. Brett looked at her with adoring eyes. Michael couldn't blame him.

"Hey Brett, it's good to see you too."

It was all Michael could manage to say under the circumstances as he struggled to keep his composure.

"So, I see you've met Rebecca," he mused, looking at her in awe. "Thanks for keeping her company. Dance clubs aren't really her scene."

It's true that she didn't seem completely comfortable in this setting, but there was no denying how much she loved to dance. She seemed completely at home on the dance floor earlier, and Michael wondered if Brett had ever seen what he had been privileged to witness tonight.

"It was my pleasure," Michael replied, looking only at Rebecca.

She smiled warmly in response until slowly the sadness returned to her eyes.

"Where is everyone else?" Brett asked, looking around the club.

"Dancing, down there," Michael gestured toward the dance floor.

Brett scanned the lower level and waved when he saw Leo. He put his arm around Rebecca's waist.

"I hope you don't mind, but I'm going to have to steal her for a little while. I never get to see her on Friday nights because she always has to work so late, and I don't want to waste the opportunity."

Her eyes were wide again as she looked back at Michael. Her whereabouts on Friday nights was obviously another piece of information she had been less-than-honest about with Brett. Michael was oddly pleased at the fact that he knew something about her that Brett didn't.

Michael gave her a knowing smile that seemed to immediately put her at ease.

"You go on ahead, I'll catch up with you later," Michael assured, in a tone that would indicate to Rebecca that it was alright with him.

He hated having to let her go, but more than anything, he didn't want her to feel any more anguish over him.

She didn't move at first when Brett took her hand, as if frozen in place. She looked as if she wanted to say something more to Michael, but couldn't. Michael wondered what she would have said if Brett hadn't interrupted them. What did she *want?* He may never know.

She reluctantly stood up. She seemed as torn as she had been two weeks ago at the top of the stairs at the bookstore café. Brett was completely oblivious, focusing on joining his friends.

As Brett and Rebecca walked away together hand in hand, her intense eyes never left Michael's. She hesitated at the top step and for a split second looked as if she would turn and come back to him.

She gave him one last gorgeous, warm smile and as Brett gently pulled her hand, she was out of sight.

As much as he wanted to stay there, to be with her a little longer, to watch her dance again, he knew it would only make it harder for both of them.

He had never really believed in love at first sight or the concept of soul mates before, but he knew now that he would never feel about anyone the way he felt about her.

It was just bad luck that Brett had gotten to her first.

The best thing he could do for her now was to leave her alone, respect her decision, and walk out the door. He resolved that he would not go back to the bookstore café, as he had promised, and in time she would go back to her weekly routine.

He fought the desire to go to the railing to have one last look at her. He didn't want her to see him leave and he wanted to remember her perfect face giving him that last warm smile.

He turned around and made his way through the crowds of admiring women, out the main entrance of the club, and down State Street toward the bookstore café.

He wanted to pass it one last time before making his way home.

# CHAPTER THREE

## *Attraction*

She woke up Saturday morning the same way she had for weeks – out of breath, her heart racing, utterly distressed, tears brimming in her eyes. The dream was always the same.

*She and Michael are together in a beautiful garden, surrounded by candlelight in each other's arms, swaying slowly to distant music. In his tender embrace, her head rests contently against his chest. She can feel his beating heart against her cheek, and can smell his heavenly scent. His strong arms around her feel safe, warm, and secure.*

*She feels utterly at peace, as if being with him makes her whole somehow. She looks up into his beautiful eyes as he gently places one finger under her chin, leaning in to kiss her. Their lips are mere millimetres from touching when they are abruptly and unwillingly pulled apart.*

*The candles slowly burn out one by one as Michael disappears into the cold darkness. She calls out for him repeatedly, frantically searching for him in the dimming light to no avail. He is nowhere to be found. Panic and sheer emptiness fill her as she wakes...*

# Behind the Glass

Despite her efforts to push him from her mind, Michael had been steadily invading her subconscious over the past three weeks since they last saw each other at the dance club.

The dreams had started that very night.

Against her better judgment, she longed to have more time with him that night. She wanted to tell him everything she truly felt about him. When she breathlessly escaped back upstairs only minutes after their coincidental encounter, he was long gone.

Filled with regret, she went back to her *hideout*, as he had called it, in the following weeks, secretly hoping in vain to see him again. To her disappointment, he had kept his promise.

Truly conflicted, she knew it was wrong to pine for him the way she did, but she couldn't deny her feelings. It was torture knowing there was someone out there whom she felt so completely in sync with. The overpowering need to be with him was unlike anything she had ever experienced before with anyone, even with Brett.

Realizing this inflicted the worst kind of guilt.

Since the day they'd met, Brett had always been a perfectly wonderful boyfriend. He was kind, attentive, romantic, and obviously enamoured with her in every way. Yet, despite his best efforts, he didn't completely understand her. They had acutely different personalities and consequentially, drastically different interests. Initially set up by Leo, they had been together for several months now, yet their relationship remained fairly idle and undeveloped.

Despite wanting more with him, she had never allowed herself to let him in completely, keeping him at a safe distance. Over the past months he had suggested moving in together a handful of times yet she always rationalized a way out of it. She always told herself that her reaction was a product of being from divorced parents, instinctually protecting herself from getting hurt. In the past few weeks, however, she began to question her motives more and more.

He normally slept at his place on Friday nights but in an effort to improve her somewhat melancholy mood lately he had surprised her last night. Most mornings she was able to deal with the aftermath of the restless nights in private, but waking up in this state today next to Brett was unsettling to say the least.

He was typically an extremely deep sleeper and wasn't ever aware of her habit of waking up in this state, but this morning was different. As she awoke today, he was laying on his side facing her, propped up on one arm. He had apparently been awake for a while watching her sleep. Caught completely off guard, she tried to read his expression hoping she hadn't been talking in her sleep.

He smiled contently, leaned in toward her, and gently kissed the top of her head.

"Good morning, Beautiful," he whispered. "Another bad dream?"

"Hi... I guess so," she muttered sleepily. "I don't really remember much. *Another?*"

She wasn't being completely dishonest. The exact details changed frequently.

"You haven't been sleeping well the last few weeks when I've spent the night. Has anything been bothering you lately?"

Other than Michael occupying her every subconscious thought?

"No, not really," she lied. "Work is a little hectic but it's nothing I can't handle."

She didn't realize Brett had noticed her restlessness for so long now.

"Maybe you should cut back a little. You work sixty hours a week, working two jobs. I'm sure Leo would let you lower your hours to three nights a week. It would also give us a little more time to spend together, besides the weekends."

For months he had been considerably patient with her, taking whatever time she was willing to give him. Virtually every free moment she had these days was spent with him. If she didn't work so much they would probably spend more time together. She didn't necessarily feel smothered by him, but she wasn't entirely used to all of the attention he paid her either.

As much as she hated to admit it, her Friday nights spent at the bookstore café *were* an escape from him. Michael had been right about that and amazingly had seen right through her that very first night.

Again, the guilt was overpowering.

"I'll give it some thought," she promised, only to appease him for the moment, "but I really need the money. My day job doesn't pay much and I need those tips."

He wrapped his arms around her and gently kissed her forehead.

"You know, if you had someone to share your expenses with you wouldn't need a second job. And I just *happen* to know someone who would be happy to do it."

It was a conversation they had had several times recently and at this moment a conversation she had no desire to repeat again. She simply didn't have the energy.

She looked lovingly into his eyes and smiled as she shrugged sheepishly. She kissed him tenderly hoping her affection would soften the blow. She had to give him credit for his patience.

"Promise me you'll think about it," he whispered in her ear.

"I will," she promised as she rested her head on his chest.

"You know you could always find another day job. Maybe something that pays more so you don't have to work nights?"

Brett had never completely understood how much she loved being a photographer and had voiced his opinion on her pay level in the past, but she wasn't going to budge on this. She felt privileged to actually have a job doing what she loved.

It was pure luck that she even had the position as a staff photographer at the *Isthmus*. After months of trying to find a job everywhere in town, with little to no professional photography experience, she coincidentally submitted her portfolio to the right person at the right time.

At the time she didn't even care what the pay was. She felt lucky to finally have the job. Until she saved enough money to go back to school, this was her education. It was gold.

"I don't really think that's an option for me. It's too important. I know it doesn't pay well, but I really do love it," she responded, slightly more poignantly than intended.

"You and your photography."

He didn't mean to sound insensitive; he just thought she sacrificed too much for her art. She found it ironic at times that the very thing she was so passionate about was totally lost on him. They had once made the mistake of going to an art opening at a gallery downtown one evening instead of the college basketball game he had opted for. Because he was utterly bored all evening, she found it impossible to truly enjoy herself.

Where she saw depth, emotion, and beauty, he saw a *picture* on a wall.

She played along with him for the moment and smiled playfully, keeping her comments to herself. She figured it was pointless to defend her feelings about art yet again.

"So it turns out I have to go into work for most of the day today. We're trying to close a deal with that company I told you about and I need to work out some details before the meeting on Monday. I'm sorry, babe. I promise I'll make it up to you. Leo and Isabel will be by this afternoon to pick you up for dinner tonight, and I'll meet you there when I'm finished."

He kissed her once more on the forehead before getting out of bed.

Brett worked for a large corporate investment firm and he had been trying to impress certain associates lately in the hopes of landing a promotion this spring. It came as no surprise to her that he would be putting in the extra time and actually welcomed a day to herself. They had planned on attending a casual dinner party at Claire's house later that evening so she would have the entire day free.

"I understand. Hopefully they'll recognize your extra effort this May."

His face lit up. It was clear that her constant support was appreciated.

"You're pretty amazing, you know that?" he asked, smiling widely as he got dressed.

"So I've been told," she teased, stretching out in the bed she planned on staying in for a while after he left. She was feeling content and extremely comfortable.

He checked his watch, clearly aware of the late morning hour. He would have normally showered and gotten ready at her place, but his spontaneous visit last night didn't come with a change of clothes. He'd have to stop back at his place before heading to the office.

After he collected his belongings, he came back to her side, gave her a long tight squeeze and a gentle yet passionate kiss. He paused for a moment before standing up to look deeply into her eyes, smiling contently.

"I love you. I'll see you tonight."

Every time he said those three words her heart sank. She tried to suppress the feelings that betrayed her, tried to convince herself it would pass in time, but ultimately over the past several weeks she realized her heart was beginning to belong to someone else.

"I love you too," she whispered, struggling to keep eye contact.

Now instead of contentment, she felt absolutely despicable.

As she watched him leave, she contemplated curling up under the covers for the rest of the day, hiding from the heart-wrenching guilt that tormented her, but thought better of it. She was stronger than that.

*Enough self-loathing,* she thought to herself.

In an effort to redirect her mind, she decided to take a long hot shower. It always relaxed her and helped wash away her anxiety. She tried to focus on anything but Michael. She was determined to get past this, to be happy with what she had, and get over what she vehemently tried to convince herself to be a temporary infatuation. For better or worse, she belonged with Brett, and she was determined to stop this subconscious infidelity, if that's what it was.

She spent the rest of her day outside around town with her beloved 35mm. It was a clear, gorgeous winter day in Madison, something somewhat rare for mid-February in Wisconsin. The temperature was still cold but moderate for this time of year. She thought it would be a shame to waste such a wonderful gift from Mother Nature on her day off.

For the remainder of the morning and most of the afternoon, she spent hours taking photo after photo of anything that caught her eye; people walking down State Street, students gathering on UW-Madison's campus, historic downtown architecture, Madison's majestic capital building, animals lounging at Henry Vilas Zoo, children playing in the snow and ice skating at Tenney Park. Her subject matter was endless.

She had been adding to her portfolio slowly over the last few months, hoping to eventually have enough material to display at a gallery one day. She figured the bookstore café would be the perfect place to start.

# Behind the Glass

She had become familiar with the owners over the past several months and almost felt comfortable testing the waters in a small gallery setting such as the bookstore. The wife was always quite friendly to her and over the past few weeks seemed more attentive in her presence.

She speculated that Michael had something to do with it and often wondered how much they knew about her. It's possible that he had mentioned her to his 'good friends,' as he had referred to them, and she wondered if he even came there anymore.

Or if she would ever see him again.

Slowly, she realized that no matter how hard she tried lately, her thoughts always seemed to lead back to him. Frustrated by this, she found it hard to concentrate on what she was doing. Even photography couldn't distract her today.

Thankfully she couldn't have been in a better place.

In the low afternoon sunlight, she sat alone on a park bench at Tenney Park looking out at Lake Mendota. Since childhood, it had been one of her favourite places to come when she needed to think, and looking out across the serene lake always brought her peace.

Reflecting on her wayward thoughts, she hoped the feelings she had for Michael would gradually fade over time. Rationally she knew it didn't make sense to be so completely captivated by someone she had spent so little time with and knew so little about. It was quite atypical for her. She didn't even know his last name.

None of that seemed to matter though. Deep down she knew everything she needed to know about him just by the way he looked at her. It was unexplainable.

Deep in thought, she sat staring out at the frozen lake for a long while until the dropping temperature reminded her what time of day it was. Evening was approaching and she had to be presentable for the upcoming gathering at Claire's. Her time at the lake had cleared her mind enough for the moment, and she resolved to pushing Michael far from her thoughts for the rest of the day, despite her unresolved feelings. Resolution would not be found today.

After stopping back home to change clothes, Leo and Isabel were a welcome distraction. It was virtually impossible to feel anything negative in their presence. They were always such an upbeat couple, full of life and so in love.

Isabel had become almost like a sister to Rebecca over the past couple of years and she had considered Leo family since before she could remember. It was always easy being with them and the car ride to Claire's house helped put her mind to rest.

"So," Isabel began, interrupting the comfortable silence in the car, "tonight should be interesting."

# Behind the Glass

"How so?" Rebecca asked casually, still looking out the window.

"Well, I guess Claire has had to work awfully hard to pull this dinner party off."

Isabel was one of the kindest hearted people Rebecca knew and would never say anything remotely negative about anyone, but due to Claire's flamboyant personality, she was sometimes the exception. Knowing this, Rebecca was vaguely intrigued.

"Really, why?"

"Well, it seems that getting together with her friends isn't the true motivation for tonight at all. Apparently she's been trying for weeks to get a date with that friend of Leo's from the dance club, Michael. She's been driving Leo crazy lately wanting information about him, his phone number, you name it. " She sounded slightly irritated.

Rebecca's heart skipped a beat, just at hearing his name. She could feel the blood rush to her face as she struggled to maintain her composure. With her senses instantly piqued, she listened to Isabel intently.

"You know how Claire gets when she finds someone she *wants*. Well he's apparently her latest obsession. I guess she's exhausted every charming proposition in her arsenal, but when she invited him to a casual get together at her house with friends, he *finally* said yes. Typical Claire."

She sighed, rolling her eyes.

Rebecca was reeling with emotion. Just as she had finally stopped thinking of him, he was going to be at the very place she had hoped would serve as a distraction. The irony was not lost on her. She couldn't decide how she felt at learning this.

One thing she *was* certain of was her feelings toward Claire.

She didn't know Claire Davenport all that well, but had been in her presence long enough to learn that she was a slightly shallow and extremely vain person. She could be dripping with sweetness one moment and then completely dismissive the next.

Claire had known Isabel for a couple of years during college and had clung to their friendship partly due to her own insecurities. Isabel, being the true saint she was, always saw the good in people and was probably Claire's only true friend. Ultimately she provided Claire with much needed confidence.

The thought of Claire pursuing Michael in this way though, made Rebecca feel an intense jealousy that was completely unexpected. Unconsciously, her jaw tightened and her adrenalin began to rise. She struggled to keep an even voice as she spoke.

"So, Claire was that taken with him after meeting him just once?"

"I guess so. Or maybe it was just his lack of interest in her that did the trick. She seems to notice anyone who doesn't notice her right away."

That was certainly true. Rebecca recalled Michael's apparent disinterest in her, despite her flirtatious advances.

Leo suddenly chuckled aloud.

"Trust me, I really don't think Claire is Michael's type," he stated bluntly.

Rebecca could always depend on Leo's brutal honesty.

"Why is that?"

"I don't know how to put this without insulting Claire, but Michael is just a very intelligent, principled... *deep* guy. No offense, but I don't see him going for a superficial blonde, that's all." He shot an apologetic look toward Isabel who smiled in response.

"You know him pretty well then?"

"Yeah, Michael and I go back a few years. He's a good guy. We were pretty close during college. I swear I wouldn't have passed some of my classes without his help. I wasn't kidding about that. He's extremely smart, and school always just came naturally to him. Each semester we'd take a couple of long weekends and go on these awesome hiking trips together. He's really into the outdoors since he was practically raised on a horse ranch, so he was a great guy to hike with. And he's an artist to boot. I swear there's not much that guy can't do."

Rebecca was digesting so much information she felt as if her head was spinning. She was grateful to Leo for filling in so many blanks, but was hanging onto one particular piece of information more than anything else.

She couldn't stop herself from asking the question.

"He's an artist?"

"Yeah. He's actually really good too, not that I'm an expert, but he's had his work displayed around town."

Things were slowly starting to fall into place.

"Really?" She tried to keep her voice even. "Would I have seen his work anywhere?"

As if she had to ask the question.

"Oh, that's right, Bec, I forgot how much you love art. Yeah, come to think of it, you know that quirky little book shop on State Street down near the Orpheum? His cousin and her husband own it and they display his art there sometimes. I think the shop is called Behind the Glass."

Rebecca sat quietly in the back seat of Leo's car as they turned onto Claire's street, lost in her own thoughts for a while. So many things went through her mind at once but the most dominant image was of the beautiful painting from the first night they had met. She smiled softly as she remembered each detail. There was no need to question or search her memory; she knew it was his. And in that moment she realized she had connected with him before they had even met, before she had looked into those soulful brown eyes.

She was speechless.

# Behind the Glass

"We're here. Are you alright?" Leo asked, looking back at Rebecca.

She struggled to snap herself out of whatever was making her mute.

"Yes, I'm fine," she whispered as she slowly got out of the car.

She concentrated on righting herself as they approached Claire's house.

Claire lived on the first floor of a large beautiful old house in an older part of Madison which had been converted into two separate dwellings. Massive stone stairs led to a huge front porch with a comfortable looking porch swing at one end. Two immense wood doors, each adorned with the letters 'A' and 'B' stood before them.

Leo knocked on the door on the left hand side.

Claire eagerly opened the door, obviously hoping to see someone other than who stood before her. Her slightly disappointed reaction told Rebecca that Michael hadn't arrived yet. This, she decided, was a good thing for the moment. She desperately needed some time to wrap her mind around several aspects of the upcoming evening.

Claire greeted everyone warmly despite her discontent. Rebecca on the other hand made an effort to be polite, trying to suppress her newfound bitterness toward her.

To no one's surprise, Jared was already there sipping a beer in the living room toward the rear of the house. Rebecca couldn't help but acknowledge the irony of his constant pursuit of Claire lately and how it was completely lost on her.

Maybe people just always want what they can't have.

They all stood casually in Claire's kitchen engaged in superficial conversation while Claire scurried back and forth preparing food. It was painfully obvious she was completely out of her element in the kitchen and it was slightly comical to watch. Isabel ultimately took pity on her and offered to help.

Rebecca tried in vain to keep her focus on the conversation and interjected comments as appropriate, but her mind was far away.

Her thoughts had taken her to Michael's painting again, to their first conversation at the bookstore, and the questions he had asked her that first night. She was realizing the answers she now had about Michael's background had only raised new ones. She found herself wondering about his childhood on the horse ranch, what his major in college was, what books he'd read, which artists he had admired and provided inspiration for his own work.

As her mind raced, she realized how much he truly intrigued her.

A knock at the front door abruptly interrupted her thoughts and Claire bounded toward the foyer. Rebecca instinctively slipped in behind everyone toward the edge of the kitchen, full of unexpected

# Behind the Glass

anxiety. She found it difficult to contain her nervousness and felt her heart begin to race.

Rebecca's view was somewhat obscured but she could see Claire opening the door and giving a flirtatious hug to who she assumed to be Michael.

Unexpected apprehension washed over Rebecca, not at seeing Michael again but at the fact she hadn't even considered that Michael may actually be interested in Claire. For some reason this possibility had completely eluded her.

As she thought this scenario through, her heart sank and she felt foolish for thinking *she* had as much of an impact on him as he surely had on her. In the past weeks he had numerous opportunities to come to the bookstore, to see her again, but he stayed away. Maybe he had accepted the fact she was with Brett and was moving on. Claire certainly was as persistent as she was beautiful when she wanted someone she felt was a challenge. Who could say no to *her*?

Secretly wishing she could escape, Rebecca glanced at the window beside her and wondered if anyone would notice her climbing out of it...

As he entered the kitchen, Michael greeted Leo with a hand shake and Isabel with a gentle hug. He stepped forward to greet Jared as Rebecca slowly slinked behind them, hoping to go unnoticed. Jared shook Michael's hand and then, as if acting on some kind of territorial instinct, crossed over to Claire, leaving Michael and Rebecca face-to-face.

She took a long shallow breath and slowly looked up at him.

He was as strikingly handsome as the first night they met, and his incredible smile almost made her tremble with emotion. Dressed in a grey button down that complimented his sculpted arms, he was clean shaven, and the subtle scent of his cologne smelled amazing. Despite her attempt of normalcy as she looked into his beautiful eyes again, she lost the ability to breathe properly and was completely tongue-tied.

On cue, he put her at ease.

"Hi, Rebecca," he said as he shook her hand, "it's good to see you again."

His tone was casual, familiar, and relaxed, as if they had known each other for years. She smiled in response and relaxed a little just at his very touch.

"Hi, Michael, it's good to see you too."

She felt more at ease and wished she could properly convey to him how wonderful it was to see him again.

"Where's Brett tonight?"

"Working... he'll be by later."

He smiled softly as he kept his eyes intently locked onto hers. A feeling of pure contentment settled around her as it had in her dreams. She couldn't deny his effect on her.

Noticing this, Claire promptly interrupted them.

# Behind the Glass

"Maybe everyone can make their way into the living room while I finish up in here. Can I get you something to drink, Michael?"

She took his hand and led him away from Rebecca into the kitchen.

As they parted, he steadily kept his eyes on Rebecca as she quietly sat down in a large leather arm chair nearest the kitchen. Leo and Isabel made themselves comfortable on the leather sofa across from her while Jared reluctantly took the second arm chair next to her. A large craftsman-style wooden coffee table sat in the middle of the space in front of a simple stone fireplace opposite the wide doorway to the kitchen.

Claire's interior decorating style was surprisingly simple, classic, and understated. Rebecca often wondered if she had it professionally decorated. It certainly contrasted from her ostentatious style in clothing, makeup, cars, and general lifestyle. Before being introduced to her exceptionally humble abode a couple years ago, Rebecca had always envisioned Claire living in the penthouse of an extravagant building downtown.

She wondered if maybe there was more to Claire than met the eye.

Rebecca was truly puzzled by Michael's presence here tonight and found herself analysing his and Claire's body language as they chatted quietly in the kitchen. Claire deliberately leaned in as she spoke, and Rebecca could swear that she saw her actually batting her eyelashes at one point.

Michael seemed genuinely polite to her when he spoke, but in a gentlemanly way, as if biding his time and keeping a safe distance. She wondered if her feelings for him were clouding her interpretations of his demeanour and tried not to over-analyse.

Later in the evening as they ate dinner, Leo, Isabel, Jared, and Claire, discussed the details of next month's upcoming wedding plans. Rebecca tried to focus on the conversation but her eyes subtly seemed to find Michael's again and again. Unnoticed by anyone else in the room, a constant volley of furtive glances existed between them.

Unintentionally interrupting this, Claire abruptly stood up.

"Oh, I forgot the bread! I'll be right back."

She hurried into the kitchen to slice the loaf of French bread she had left on the counter. As she sliced, she kept a watchful eye on Michael as if claiming her territory. Rebecca normally wouldn't have noticed this, but the sharp glances she was getting from Claire all evening made it more apparent. Claire's lack of self-confidence constantly surprised Rebecca.

"Aaahhh, dammit!" Claire gasped aloud.

"What is it Claire?" Isabel asked, as she arose from her seat at the table.

Claire, being so distracted with watching Michael, hadn't been paying attention to what she was doing and had sliced her finger with the serrated bread knife.

Isabel's nursing instinct took over and she was at Claire's side in a moment assessing the wound. The cut was deep and blood was quickly dripping off her finger, saturating the wooden cutting board along with the bread atop it. Isabel wrapped a clean towel around the wound and applied pressure as she shot a quick glance to Leo.

"It's a deep cut, sweetie. It looks like you're going to need stitches. We should probably take you to the Emergency Room." Isabel had a sweet, motherly tone.

"No, it's not that bad. The ER? I'm fine, really. I'm sure it will close up and stop bleeding in no time," Claire whined in a panicked voice.

"It's not a clean cut though, honey, and the knife you used had a serrated edge. It's deep and it's going to keep bleeding. Please let Leo and I take you. Maybe I can get things moving a little faster in the ER since I know some of the doctors there."

Claire furrowed her eyebrows and pursed her lips in a pout. She looked down at the blue towel that was slowly turning a deep shade of purple and finally, after contemplating leaving Michael, conceded by nodding her head. Predictably, vanity took over. The thought of having a nasty scar on her perfectly manicured fingers was likely too much to bear.

"Fine, let's go," she pouted, "but what about dinner?"

"We were almost finished anyway and I'm sure Rebecca won't mind cleaning up for you. We'll do dessert and coffee another night, okay?"

Before Claire could argue, Leo was at her side leading her to the front door. Looking over her shoulder, her eyes frantically tried to find Michael's as they approached the foyer. She gestured a wave with her good hand and he gave her a polite smile in return before they were gone.

Rebecca, Michael, and Jared were left standing around the small island in the kitchen in an uncomfortable silence.

Rebecca impulsively began cleaning the blood-stained cutting board. She figured the best way to calm her nerves was to keep busy. She threw the bread in the garbage and rinsed the cutting board in the sink.

"You're not going with them?" Jared asked Michael.

Michael seemed surprised by the question.

"No, I think I'll help Rebecca clean up."

"Well, I'm going," Jared declared.

"Suit yourself," Michael replied, smiling with a raised eyebrow. He seemed slightly amused at Jared's tone.

"Fine. I'll see you two later."

Jared walked eagerly toward the front door. It was ironic that his constant pursuit of whom he desired was matched only by Claire's.

# Behind the Glass

Rebecca continued to methodically wash dishes, unsure of what to expect next.

This very moment was something she had been secretly dreaming about for weeks, yet this was the last scenario in the world she had anticipated. Through a series of bizarre circumstances, she and Michael were now finally alone together.

She could feel his eyes on her from across the room and wanted to turn around to face him, but had no idea what she would say. She had a multitude of questions for him and her emotions ran wild just being alone in his presence again.

Luckily, after a few moments, he made the first move.

He slowly crossed the kitchen to where she stood and paused directly behind her. She stopped washing the pot in her hand and slowly closed her eyes, inhaling his wonderful scent. She could feel his body heat at her back as her heart raced.

He stood in place for a few moments before he spoke and she wondered what he would do or say next. The sheer anticipation gave her goose bumps.

"I..." She flinched slightly as his voice broke the silence. "I'll get the dishes from the dining room for you."

Clearly struggling with restraint himself, he reluctantly walked into the adjacent room, collected a handful of dishes, and brought them to the counter next to her. He took another step closer and stopped next to her, just inches away. She could feel his eyes on her again, as her heart pounded.

She turned off the water and faced him, her eyes slowly looking up into his. She had once again forgotten how much taller he was. His massive stature, his very presence near her, made her heart race with anticipation. Quietly looking down at her, he smiled.

There were an infinite number of things to say to him at this moment but nothing immediately came to mind. All she could do was smile up at him contently.

Pure happiness filled her heart.

"So..." he began.

Before she could stop herself, she interrupted him mid-sentence.

"Why are you here?" she asked softly, unable to release herself from his powerful gaze. The way he looked at her seemed to be affecting her normally logical thought process. This was apparently the first question that popped into her mind and now, impossible to retract.

"Here in the kitchen?" he teased, smiling.

"Here at Claire's house," she clarified.

He sighed and looked down for a moment, then back at her.

"Weakness on my part," he admitted.

Claire's persistence had obviously worked.

"She's hard to resist, I suppose," she rolled her eyes slightly.

He gave her a confused look.

"Who?"

"Claire. She can be incredibly tenacious."

She had to give Claire credit for knowing just how to use her alluring ways to get what she wanted.

His puzzled expression softened into a smile, as if something amused him. He shook his head and chuckled softly.

"Why are you laughing?"

She felt as if she had missed the punch line to a joke.

"You."

"Me? What about me?"

"Rebecca, I didn't come here tonight... for *Claire*."

His expression slowly became more serious, more intense as he spoke.

She took a moment to respond as what he had said sunk in.

She furrowed her brow in confusion.

"Oh, I..." she trailed off, unsure of what to say next.

"I've tried to stay away from you, Rebecca. *Believe me*, I've tried. But tonight, like I said, I had a moment of weakness." He locked eyes with her again.

As she slowly thought this through, something occurred to her.

"But, what about the bookstore?"

A look of genuine conflict crossed his face.

"I promised to leave you alone, to let you have your place to escape. It took *all* of my will power to stay away, knowing you were there." He looked down after he spoke.

"So, why now? Why here?" she asked, hoping he would look at her again.

"Like you said, Claire's persistence is... impressive, and I couldn't seem to stop myself from coming knowing you would be here. I'm sorry," he said, as his eyes met hers again.

"*You're* sorry?" she sighed, realizing the irony of the situation.

As she looked at him, images of her dreams filled her mind, followed by the intense guilt from this morning and for what she felt at this moment. She couldn't deny the unexplainable completeness she felt when they were together, and she knew it was unlike anything she had experienced with Brett. It wasn't until she met Michael that she truly understood the difference. She also knew she simply didn't have it in her to be unfaithful to Brett or to break his heart. Her personal principles forbade it. She would never adequately be able to convey how sorry *she* was.

She could feel the sudden tears brimming in her eyes, betraying her.

"I shouldn't have come. It was selfish. The last thing I wanted to do was upset you. Please forgive me."

As he spoke, he automatically brushed his hand over her cheek, comforting her.

His very touch sent unexpected shivers down her spine and made her tremble slightly. She lightly caught her breath as she unconsciously leaned upward toward him. It seemed the closer they were to each other the more intensely drawn to him she became. At this moment, her actions were admittedly somewhat out of her control.

In response, his grip became slightly firmer and his hand moved back toward her neck. He leaned in slowly, trying to control himself but she was quickly moving in toward him at the same time. Their faces remained inches apart for what felt like an eternity, neither of them daring to cross the line.

They gazed deeply into each other's eyes until finally Michael closed his and gently kissed her forehead. She closed her eyes at the gentle touch of his lips to her skin. Slowly their hands naturally found each other as they stood with only their foreheads touching for several minutes until Rebecca finally spoke.

"I can't," she whispered with tears streaming down her face.

"I know," he whispered back, "it's okay." His voice was amazingly soothing.

*This,* however, was *anything* but okay, and Rebecca desperately wished she could stay here with him like this forever. She had never felt conflict like this in her life. She wished she could put her conscience on hold and think with her heart instead of her head for once. She realized all too clearly that her dream had become reality.

As if on cue, a knock at the front door interrupted them.

They both flinched guiltily and took a step back from each other. Rebecca quickly wiped the tears from her face as she tried to compose herself. Michael sighed and gave her a long solemn look before he turned toward the foyer to answer the door.

Rebecca turned the water back on and continued to wash dishes, desperately trying to calm her mind and body. Her hands were still shaking slightly as she fumbled with each dish. She frantically tried to remember a simple breathing exercise she had learned in yoga class that always helped her focus.

Michael, who outwardly seemed completely at ease, opened the door and greeted Brett with a handshake. Rebecca was thankful for his ability to keep it together and wished she could do the same.

Unaware of the intense emotional atmosphere he had just walked into, Brett was as upbeat as always. His inattention to detail was a blessing at the moment.

"Hey, man, where is everyone else? I didn't see many cars out front," Brett asked as he came inside and closed the door.

Michael didn't miss a beat.

"Claire sliced her finger with a bread knife. The cut was pretty deep, so Leo and Isabel took her to the ER," he explained casually, leading him toward the kitchen.

"You're kidding! That's too bad. And Jared? Oh wait, let me guess. He went too?"

It was amazing how everyone had picked up on Jared's behaviour except Claire.

"Yeah, he did. Rebecca and I have been cleaning up from dinner."

He gestured toward Rebecca.

Brett's face lit up the moment he saw Rebecca across the kitchen washing dishes.

She took a deep breath and turned her head in Brett's direction. She smiled as cheerfully as she could manage, but the moment their eyes met and she saw the sweet devotion in his gaze, her stomach began to twist and turn.

"Hey, baby," he said as he walked to her side and placed his hand on the small of her back. "I'm sorry I missed dinner. We had a lot more prep work than I thought we would have and I had to stay and help finish everything up for Monday."

"That's okay."

She turned off the water and dried her hands on a towel. He gave her a soft kiss and a tight hug.

"I missed you," he whispered in her ear. As she hugged him, she looked over his shoulder at Michael and quickly closed her eyes, unable to bear looking at him.

She gently released herself from his embrace and smiled sweetly.

"I should probably finish cleaning and package up that food," she said, pointing to the uneaten leftovers on the counter. She desperately hoped kitchen clean-up duty would serve as a distraction, and that Brett wouldn't notice how unbelievably uncomfortable she was at the moment.

As if reading her mind, Michael began casually chatting about college basketball scores and upcoming games with Brett as he handed Rebecca plastic containers he found for the food. Once Brett was sufficiently engrossed in the conversation, he shot Rebecca a playful smile that immediately put her at ease.

She smiled gratefully in response.

After all of the dishes were cleaned and all of the food put away neatly in the refrigerator, Rebecca made her way into the living room where Brett and Michael were still talking. As far as she could tell, they were reminiscing over a hiking story during college involving Leo doing something foolish. She smiled politely as she sat next to Brett, but wasn't even listening to a word they were saying. She was still much too distracted and tense to converse coherently.

Thankfully they didn't seem to notice her silence.

"Well, it's getting late and I actually haven't eaten dinner yet," Brett said as he looked at Rebecca, "Will you let me take you out for an apology dessert while I get a bite to eat?"

As much as she wanted to prolong her time with Michael, she actually welcomed any excuse to end this uncomfortable evening.

"Sure, that would be nice." She struggled to keep an even voice.

Michael slowly stood up.

"I should be heading home, too. It was good catching up with you, man. It's been a long time."

"You too, Michael. We'll see you next month at the wedding though, right?"

He took Rebecca's hand and led her toward the front door.

It was something that hadn't even occurred to Rebecca. Of course Michael would have been invited. Leo and Isabel wanted a small wedding, but surely he would be there as one of Leo's close friends. She found herself fighting the urge to smile and felt nervous butterflies at the thought of being able to see him again.

Then as she looked at Brett, she clenched her teeth with shame.

"Yes, you will. I'm looking forward to it," he replied, glancing momentarily at Rebecca, "Leo and Isabel finally getting married has been a long time coming."

Brett smiled widely, "Didn't he tell us he was going to marry her after their first date or something?"

"After their first conversation, I think."

"Well, we'll see you at the wedding then," Brett said as they all walked out the front door together onto the huge front porch.

Michael turned off the lights and made sure the door was locked behind them as they exited.

Rebecca couldn't help but take notice of how considerate Michael was. All evening, in any given situation, he seemed to always do the most honourable and appropriate thing. She realized it was probably the most attractive and appealing characteristic about him – he was just innately *good.*

The three made their way to their vehicles and just as Brett opened the door for Rebecca, Michael looked back at them.

"It was good to see you again, Rebecca. Have a good evening, okay?"

He looked at her with kind, caring eyes as if wanting to make sure she would be alright. Brett had been oblivious to her behaviour since his arrival but she knew Michael had picked up on the fact that she was on the edge of falling apart.

As always, she was instantly at ease when he looked at her this way. All of the conflicted emotions she felt melted away with his amazingly warm smile.

"I will, thank you."

She smiled and was grateful that this goodbye was less painful than the previous partings they'd had.

He gave her one last warm look as he got into his black truck and slowly drove away. As she sat in

# Behind the Glass

Brett's car, she watched his truck drive down Claire's street until it turned down a side street and was out of sight.

She barely noticed that Brett had been talking to her and as if coming out of a daze, slowly turned to him to focus on what he was saying.

"So, what do you say, are you ready to hit the town with me?"

No, not at all actually. What she wanted to do was curl up and hide for a while, to not think about anyone or anything, to not feel this way anymore. Hitting the town was quite possibly the last thing in the world she wanted to do at the moment.

So naturally, she lied.

"Let's go!" she agreed, smiling as widely as she could bear.

# CHAPTER FOUR

*Desire*

The drive up north took longer than even Michael had predicted. The snow had been falling steadily all day and the roads were down to one lane already. Even in his sturdy four-wheel-drive truck he couldn't make the trip go any faster. Traffic on the highway was practically at a standstill.

He wasn't worried about the time though. He had allowed plenty of leeway for the road conditions and was confident he'd make the wedding with time to spare. The ceremony was scheduled to start at six o'clock, which was over four hours away.

After so many months filled with meticulous planning and anticipation, Leo and Isabel's wedding was finally taking place tonight, on a Friday evening, at one of their favourite venues in the world. It was the first place Leo and Isabel had vacationed together and the site of his romantic marriage proposal months ago. It seemed only fitting that they had the ceremony there as well.

Together, their families rented an entire bed and breakfast resort in central Wisconsin for the occasion. The Winterbloom Inn was an incredibly picturesque spot, located two hours north of Madison near a charming little town called Wild Rose. Its one hundred twenty acres of scenic countryside composed of hills, woods, and valleys made it immensely popular during the summer months. Its grounds included miles of private hiking trails, waterfalls, ponds, and beautiful gardens.

Due to its close proximity to several ski lodges surrounding Nordic Mountain just a few miles away, the Winterbloom was one of the few bed and breakfasts in the area that stayed open year-round. In addition to their summer vacations there, Leo and Isabel also loved escaping there to ski during the winter months. Coincidentally, Michael had come there with his family several times throughout his childhood and adult life and he actually knew the place quite well.

The main section of the inn was comprised of five bungalow style buildings reflecting the Arts & Crafts style of the early 1900's. The largest of the bungalows contained the main lobby, a moderately sized dining room, a large hall used for wedding ceremonies and the like, complete with a grand staircase, and on the opposite side of the building, a large reception hall that opened out to the majestic landscape beyond.

Three smaller buildings housed individual guest suites, each unique in Craftsman style, and the smallest cottage housed the elegant and extremely private honeymoon suite. All of the buildings except the honeymoon suite were connected by covered walkways adorned with trellis and vines that bloomed in the spring and summer.

The couple had planned their wedding in early March so their families, who had become quite close over the years, could enjoy a fun skiing weekend with them before they ventured to Maui for their two week honeymoon.

However, the current weather conditions had not been in their plans. Heavy snow storms in Wisconsin during this time of year certainly were not unheard of, but in this case, quite unwelcome. But Michael had a feeling that Leo and Isabel were too happy to even notice.

As he finally reached the exit which led to the back roads to the inn, Michael sighed in relief, partly due to the more acceptable speed he would finally be able to keep, but mostly because each mile he travelled brought him closer to Rebecca.

Being away from her over the past couple of weeks had been difficult, and the anticipation of what he resolved to be their last time together was almost unbearable.

More than anything in the world, he longed to see her one last time.

After witnessing how much anguish he had caused her at Claire's house, he had made peace with the fact that he could no longer go on this way, torturing her the way he did. As remarkable as it was to be with her in those few amazing moments, and as satisfying as it was to truly know how real their intense connection was, he hated the fact that he had caused her so much conflict and heartache. After this last encounter at the wedding, he planned to leave her alone for good and let her get back to the life she had chosen with Brett.

Ironically, the love he felt for her and his need to see her happy had given him the strength he needed to let her go.

As he drove on through the snowy side roads, memories of their last encounter filled his mind. Recalling each detail, he pictured her smile, her expressive emerald eyes, and her long flowing caramel hair. He basked in the memory of her intoxicatingly fragrant scent and the unbelievably soft skin he had been lucky enough to kiss with his lips and hold in his hands.

After tonight these memories of her would have to be enough for him. Causing her more pain was simply not an option. As he recalled the look in her eyes that night at having to say no to him, he vowed to never put her in that position again. He decided to make the upcoming days as easy for her as possible by keeping a safe distance and watching her from afar.

For *her*, the only person he would ever love this way, it was an easy sacrifice to make.

After finally arriving at the inn and settling into his room, Michael decided to explore the main building before the ceremony began. He rationalized that it was completely appropriate to be social and mingle with the other guests, but deep down he secretly hoped to catch even the smallest glimpse of Rebecca by chance.

To no one's surprise, the guest list was quite small. No more than sixty chairs stood in a traditional arrangement in the middle of the main hall. Leo's family was extremely well-connected and seemed to know virtually everyone in Madison. However, Leo and Isabel had insisted on keeping the number down and limiting the guest list to close friends and family. They feared it would quickly turn into a circus if they didn't put their foot down.

In reality, Leo would have opted for eloping but he knew how Isabel had always dreamed of a fairy-tale wedding, and simply couldn't deny her.

Isabel revelled in the planning of this day and paid close attention to each detail, making it as elegant a wedding as she could. She insisted on keeping the decorations to a minimum due to the location. The building's natural historic beauty left little to be improved upon and it was truly a charming setting on its own.

The perimeter of the large hall and the railings of the grand staircase were adorned simply with a garland of ferns and white lilies, Isabel's favourite flower. Two moderately-sized flower arrangements full of more white lilies and dark blue violets stood at each side of the base of the staircase.

A taller, larger arrangement stood at the front of the hall where the ceremony was to take place. Large ornate candelabras stood at the center point of each of the four immense windows on the wall opposite the staircase, and an intricate chandelier hung in the center of the two-story space.

As the ceremony grew closer, guests casually made their way to their seats and voices gradually began to soften. A cellist and violinist played softly in the background as the lights slowly dimmed. The fragrant lilies and surrounding candlelight set a perfectly romantic tone as the big moment approached.

Michael had to give Isabel and Leo credit for creating a flawless setting.

The angelic music faded slowly until it stopped completely. Within a couple of seconds every voice in the main hall was utterly silent. After a few moments, Pachelbel's "Canon" began to play as people turned and faced the rear of the room, all eyes on the grand staircase.

The bridesmaids and groomsman entered the room first, each through two arched openings located on either side of the staircase. Leo's cousin, Drew and Isabel's sister, Corin, were the first couple to emerge from the entrances and walk slowly into position, followed by Jared and Claire.

Michael couldn't help but notice the victoriously happy grin on Jared's face at finally having Claire on his arm as they passed him, and of course Claire's typically provocative glance in his direction.

He was actually somewhat amazed at her tenacity after so many of her phone messages over the past couple of weeks had gone unanswered. He truly hoped to keep his interactions with her to a minimum tonight.

After weeks of patiently waiting for this moment, Rebecca finally appeared from one of the arched entrances, walking slowly to Brett and taking his arm at the base of the main staircase.

To describe her as simply *beautiful* was a vast understatement. She was a vision.

She wore a simply designed midnight blue strapless satin gown that curved perfectly with her delicate figure and flared out slightly toward the bottom. Having only seen her in ordinary winter clothes, he was stunned at how flawless and unbelievably appealing her soft ivory skin looked against the colour of the dress.

Her beautiful bronze hair was partially pulled back into a rhinestone hairpiece atop her head and gently flowed down her back in elegant ringlets. She wore a simple pearl and diamond necklace and matching teardrop earrings, and for the first time since Michael had known her, she wore a hint of makeup on her face.

Michael had always been of the opinion that her naturally perfect face didn't need anything to improve it, but was surprised at how stunning the makeup made her look.

She literally took his breath away.

Letting her go tonight would be more difficult than even he had anticipated.

# Behind the Glass

As she and Brett walked down the aisle together, Michael purposely slipped in behind another guest, out of her sight line. He figured that being as little a distraction to her as possible during the ceremony was the least he could do for her. As he made sure she couldn't see him, he never once took his eyes off of her.

Once the wedding party was in place, including Leo who looked incredibly dapper in his tuxedo, the music faded and Wagner's wedding march filled the hall. Every set of eyes in the audience locked onto Isabel at once as she emerged at the top of the staircase on her father's arm and glided slowly down step by step, looking completely radiant and smiling as wide as ever.

As her eyes met Leo's, it was instantly apparent to every single person in the room that the entire world had gradually faded away for both of them, and that in this moment, they only saw each other.

Michael could relate to this feeling completely.

He barely paid attention to the ceremony, or to the vows, or to what the minister was saying about marriage, or to anything else for that matter. All he saw was Rebecca.

She smiled proudly as she watched her best friends exchange vows. She appeared carelessly happy and unburdened. It was wonderful to see her this way, a welcome contrast to their last encounter.

She wiped a tear from her eye and smiled in excitement as they repeated their 'I dos' and concluded the ceremony with a deeply heartfelt kiss. Michael imagined it must have been like seeing a brother get married from Rebecca's perspective, and it was touching to see the unique bond they shared.

As they were joyfully pronounced 'Man and Wife,' the guests erupted in applause, and for one brief moment, Michael caught Rebecca's eye. He had hoped to remain hidden until the reception but the look on her face confirmed that she had seen him.

Her expression surprised him though. Instead of her usual look of shock, she smiled contently as if relieved to finally see him again. As they looked at one another they shared a familiar smile as if saying *hello.* Michael was both relieved and pleased by this, and hoped her happiness would continue. It would certainly make their final parting easier to bear.

After Leo and Isabel happily made their way down the aisle as a married couple, and Rebecca and Brett slowly followed behind them, her beautiful, longing eyes never left Michael's until the wedding party was out of sight.

The look in her eyes was unlike anything Michael had ever seen before. Not unlike Claire's trademark glares, this look was one of pure, unbridled *desire.*

Without warning, all logical thought vanished from his mind and he instantly felt drunk with euphoria, hopelessly under her spell.

He couldn't rationally explain why he was so drawn to her, why looking into her eyes sent him reeling with emotion in a way he'd never experienced before, or why it took all of his strength and willpower to stay away from her, but there was no denying her effect on him.

It was as if she was a forbidden drug and he was completely, hopelessly, and impetuously addicted. He found himself at a moral crossroads with his emotions completely out of balance as he made his way out of the main hall into the reception area. It was difficult to think rationally.

He wondered if he could last the weekend in her presence without acting on his feelings for her. Was it too late to change his plan of keeping his distance and letting her go?

He wondered if he was even strong enough or if he would lose control in a moment of weakness. It certainly would be next to impossible to control these impulses with *that look* in those beautiful eyes staring back at him.

As he wrestled with these new feelings, he glanced at the door leading outside. The best thing he could do right now was to walk out the door, take a few minutes to clear his mind, and get some perspective.

It seemed to be an acceptable alternative to a cold shower at the moment.

As he began walking toward the door, he was inconveniently interrupted.

"Hey, Michael!" a female voice called from a distance. Claire's timing was uncanny.

He stopped in his tracks, contemplating how rude it would be to run out the door.

Slowly, he turned to face the music, as it were.

"Hi Claire, it's good to see you again." He kept his tone perfectly even.

"Hey, stranger!" she purred as she lightly grabbed his arm, "I'm so glad to see you. I've been trying to reach you and left you a couple of messages last week but I guess you never got them. I wanted to see if you'd like to go out again sometime. My dinner party didn't exactly end the way I had planned," she raised her finger with a small bandage wrapped around it. Clearly after two weeks she was still milking everything she could out of her tiny injury.

It took all of Michael's self-control not to roll his eyes.

"Yes, I imagine a trip to the ER wasn't much fun. How's your finger?"

"Well, it's much better now, but I had to have four stitches. They say it won't leave much of a scar and..." Michael stopped listening after a while and scanned the room for Rebecca. If Claire had gotten away from the wedding party, maybe she had too.

He had no idea what to expect tonight, from her or himself. He decided that for the time being he would simply play it by ear, keep his distance, and try to control his emotions and himself.

Still, he couldn't get *the look* she had given him out of his mind.

# Behind the Glass

After listening to Claire drone on about every detail of her emergency room experience, Michael politely excused himself and headed toward the men's room. He figured it was the one place he'd be completely safe from her. She was truly becoming exhausting to deal with.

Willing himself to focus, he splashed some cool water onto his face and stared into the mirror. He tried to snap out of whatever it was that threw logic and ethics out the window where Rebecca was concerned.

He took a deep breath, trying to recall his reasons for letting her go.

As immoral as it was, the desire to be with her seemed to be amplified by what he thought he saw in her eyes. It was easier to let her go if she appeared to be committed to her decision, but now he wasn't entirely sure of her feelings. This newfound uncertainty was sheer torture.

Michael walked back into the reception hall just as Leo and Isabel were being announced. Thankfully, this meant the wedding party was present as well. He searched the room until he finally found Rebecca sitting at a table on the opposite side, talking to Brett. Her back was to him so she hadn't seen him yet. This, he decided, was a good thing.

Sticking to the original plan for the moment, he took a seat at the nearest table and tried to blend in. He made small talk with some of the other guests, but was always acutely aware of Rebecca's every move.

Leo and Isabel were enjoying their first dance together looking happier than he'd ever seen them. When the other guests were invited to join them on the dance floor he watched as Brett took Rebecca's hand and gently led her in a variation of a waltz. Under the soft lighting that surrounded them, she looked simply radiant. She floated along with the music, completely relaxed. Seeing her dance again was an unexpected treat.

Simply put, she was an angel.

He became completely fixated on her, failing to notice Claire eagerly charging toward him. She had finished her obligatory dance with Jared, and was candidly taking the opportunity to ask Michael. He was totally unprepared and had nowhere to run.

"Hey, you," she flirted, "would you be kind enough to join me on the dance floor?"

Before he could even answer she was taking his hand and pulling him out of his chair. He considered resisting for a moment, but thought better of it. Better to keep a low profile and not cause a scene. It was only one dance.

Trying to contain his annoyance, they danced on the opposite end of the dance floor from Rebecca. Claire continuously tried to dance inappropriately close to him, but Michael politely kept a gentlemanly distance. If they were anywhere else he would have abruptly ended this type of behaviour by simply walking away, but for now he had to endure her ridiculous advances and be cordial for a while longer.

As the song changed he saw Rebecca switch partners to dance with Leo. She gave Leo the same familiar smile Michael had observed many times before, and as Leo whispered something into her ear, she laughed sweetly.

Michael also noticed Brett excuse himself and head toward one of the entrances. As much as he hated to admit it, he was oddly relieved at his temporary absence.

Leo and Rebecca continued to laugh and chat throughout the dance as they slowly made their way around the dance floor. Slowly, Michael and Claire's dancing path subtly meandered toward them.

As much as he had tried to blend in and stay away from her, her sheer proximity blurred the line between right and wrong. He was admittedly not entirely in control of his own actions, and seemed to be having another moment of weakness.

Eventually the two couples approached each other. Leo's eye caught Michael's.

"Hey Michael, sorry I haven't had a chance to say hello to you yet," he said, shaking Michael's hand. "It's so good to see you here, man. Thanks for making the trip up in this horrendous weather."

Michael and Rebecca shared a friendly smile for a fraction of a second.

"I wouldn't have missed it for the world. Congratulations!"

"Thanks! Yeah, it really went off without a hitch. Isabel's amazing!"

"And now she's all yours," Michael joked.

"You better believe it!" he declared, smiling widely. "Hey, man, I'll definitely catch up with you later. But right now, *this* bridesmaid still owes me a dance!" he announced, smiling directly at Claire.

Claire, looking truly torn, slowly left Michael's side to join Leo in a dance she could not refuse at the moment. As Leo eventually led her away from them, Claire stared after Michael.

Michael was eternally grateful to Leo.

Without hesitation, Michael held out his hand to Rebecca and smiled.

Her casual demeanour quickly evolved into nervousness as she took his hand. Being as respectful as possible, he carefully placed his hand on her lower back and slowly pulled her closer. Her body became slightly rigid as they began dancing and she avoided eye contact, which was actually quite natural given their height difference.

After a little while she relaxed slightly and finally looked up at him.

"I'm sorry. I'm not very good at this," she admitted timidly.

He now regretted putting her in yet another unexpected situation with him that made her uncomfortable. So much for sticking to the plan of keeping a distance.

Still, he couldn't deny how wonderful it was to have her in his arms again.

"What is that exactly?"

Maybe he could do something to help put her at ease.

"Dancing," she replied to his sheer surprise.

He sighed in relief and smiled widely.

"You're worried about your dancing skills?"

"Yes. I'm just glad you're leading."

She seemed almost embarrassed and self-conscious but in an adorable way.

He couldn't help but be utterly amused at her priorities at the moment. She was as unpredictable as always.

"I'd have to disagree with you wholeheartedly," he argued sarcastically.

Her confused expression gradually transformed into slight embarrassment. She had obviously forgotten about the dance club.

"Oh, that's right," she recalled, cringing. "Well, you must be biased then."

He was continuously surprised at how she saw herself. Simply absurd.

"Well, yes, I definitely am, but trust me, I wasn't the only one to notice you. You really should give yourself more credit."

She smiled humbly, conceding to his compliments.

"Thank you. I guess I'm just not used to..."

"People admiring your beauty?"

As he spoke he surveyed every inch of her face.

For a moment she felt slightly faint in his arms and her face flushed red.

"No... just you."

She looked at him for a short while without a word. He desperately wondered what was going through her mind as her expression slowly evolved into the same look of desire he had witnessed earlier. He felt an unexpected shiver down his back and seriously considered whisking her away at that very moment.

Luckily for both of them, she slowly looked down, composed herself and purposely changed the subject.

"So, I'm curious about something."

Her apprehensive tone made him wonder.

"What about?"

"Leo told me you were an artist."

At times he was genuinely fascinated with her thought process. This was quite possibly the last thing in the world he expected her to say. He was unprepared, but had a feeling where the conversation would lead.

He answered carefully.

"Among other things, yes I am."

He kept his answer purposely vague. The next question was inevitable.

"Why didn't you tell me that first night?" she asked, locking eyes with him.

"That I was an artist?"

"That the painting I was going on and on about was yours."

She was perceptive. There was no point in denying it at this point.

"Would it have made a difference?"

"No, not about my opinion of the painting, but..." she stopped herself mid-sentence and smiled. "I would have enjoyed knowing it was yours. You're extremely talented, you know."

She looked back at him with the warmest, most beautiful eyes he had ever seen, and he couldn't adequately process what he was feeling. Memories of that first night flooded his mind and he felt absolutely content.

"Thank you," he finally said. "I'm sorry I didn't tell you it was mine. You were just so passionately defending the talent of the artist of the month, and spoke so highly of the painting, that at a certain point it would have been awkward to mention it. I didn't want to risk embarrassing you. It had taken me weeks to work up the nerve to even talk to you, and the last thing I wanted to do was make a mistake like that."

Her jaw unconsciously dropped open slightly as she looked at him. He couldn't read her expression but she seemed somewhat stunned. He couldn't understand why.

"Weeks?" she whispered. He could barely make out what she had said.

"What was that?"

"You said it took you *weeks* to talk to me?"

Had he really just admitted that to her? He tried to recall. Obviously he had.

He cringed internally. Too late now...

"You caught that. I'm sorry. I seem to excel at making you uncomfortable."

He was now feeling a bit uncomfortable himself. As usual his unfiltered thoughts seemed to flow freely in her presence and he hoped he hadn't said too much.

"Please, don't apologize. You don't make me feel uncomfortable, not at all. It's just the opposite actually. I feel more comfortable than I ever have in my life when I'm with you. It's amazing that you don't even realize the effect you have on me. You just have no idea..." she stopped herself as if she had said too much.

Her expression changed drastically as she spoke. The look of sheer longing in her gorgeous green eyes surprised even Michael. Instinctively, he pulled her closer to him. He was careful not to cross certain lines though, given where they were and who could be watching.

"Trust me, I know," he whispered in her ear.

They danced slowly together without a word for a while. His mind raced as he contemplated every possible scenario and weighed what was right versus what he wanted. He could easily see himself doing a number of things they would both regret, but knew in the end he would ultimately do the right thing, no matter how much he wanted her. Ironically, he knew she felt the same exact way.

For now he would simply enjoy the time they had together. Their feelings were strong now, but they would fade over time and eventually be distant memories.

As he held her close, he inhaled her sweet scent and gazed at her radiantly beautiful face. In this moment, as she looked up at him, he felt remarkably lucky. If nothing else, at least they would have this memory of each other.

As the music changed again, they slowly made their way off of the dance floor together. She led him by the hand toward a grouping of tables, stopped, and turned around to look at him. Her mood seemed to be thoughtful and reflective.

"Stay right there. I'll be right back." She seemed to be contemplating something.

He wasn't sure what she was thinking but agreed, trusting her.

"Should I be worried?" he teased.

"No, not at all. I just have to go get something. I won't be long, I promise."

She headed toward one of the entrances and stopped momentarily to look back at him before exiting the room. She smiled with focused, determined eyes as if taking in every moment of this evening.

Naturally, he smiled in response, but realized he disliked seeing her go.

After a brief moment she turned around, and headed down the hall out of sight.

As always, she was a total mystery. He had to give her credit for always keeping him guessing and surprising him at every turn. He loved that about her. It was anyone's guess as to what she was up to right now and his mind instinctively began to wonder.

He couldn't imagine where she would be going so promptly, or what she possibly needed to retrieve. He had a few random theories, but felt as though he was missing something. Something in her eyes gave him reason to wonder, and he pondered why she had looked back at him the way she had.

As he remembered the last expression on her face, something slowly started occurring to him. Something he maybe didn't want to realize. As this hypothesis began to solidify, he couldn't be sure if what he was now considering was real or imagined. His continued uncertainty seemed to be clouding his judgment.

He wondered if she was merely making an excuse to leave the reception. She *had* told him to stay there and that she would be right back, but had that last look been... an invitation? He wondered if he was somehow surreptitiously trying to get him alone.

Again his thoughts drifted to that first delicious look of desire.

He couldn't be sure of anything, but his need to be with her was definitely blocking all rational thought. He pondered several other possibilities for her behaviour, and tried to think logically, but couldn't shake the feeling he would be missing out on a unique opportunity if he simply stayed there.

The worst case scenario would be that he was wrong about her intentions. If that was the case, he could easily fake needing to use the men's room. At the very least, he could take a casual stroll around the reception hall and meander in that direction while he waited.

He shook his head smiling.

It was amazing how easily he could talk himself into anything where she was concerned, as immoral as it was. Admittedly he wasn't as strong as he had thought.

Aware of each passing minute, he could feel an irresistible pull in her direction building and wondered how much regret he would endure in the years to come if he didn't go to her this minute.

A part of him also yearned to know her true feelings.

As he struggled with what to do next, he caught sight of what would ultimately make his decision for him out of the corner of his eye.

Before Claire even reached the edge of the dance floor, he was gone.

# CHAPTER FIVE

*Cheater*

Rebecca's pace was faster than normal as she walked down the long corridor. Aware of every passing minute, she knew she had very little time to waste. In these next hours, time would be of the essence.

She tried to slow to a more natural gait, concentrating on not tripping in her heels and flowing bridesmaid dress, but her adrenalin level was building by the moment. Being in his exquisite presence again had dramatically affected her, both physically and emotionally, and it was strangely invigorating.

Acknowledging the painful fact that this would ultimately be their last time together, she had resolved to make the best of every single second with him. If nothing else, she would allow herself this *one last thing*.

It had occurred to her while dancing with Michael earlier that she had promised Leo and Isabel a collection of tasteful black and whites for their wedding album. Her window of opportunity to preserve the memory of him had finally presented itself, and she could not pass it up. She had decided right then and there that if she couldn't be with him, she certainly would never let herself forget him. Ever.

# Behind the Glass

As she finally approached the doorway to the coatroom to retrieve her camera bag, she slowed her stride slightly, but her momentum didn't idle until she was well inside the room. Filled with restless anticipation she quickly surveyed the wall of shelves before her, scanning for her dark blue camera bag. She finally found it buried behind several large handbags.

As she eagerly grabbed it and began heading for the door, she unexpectedly heard muffled noises and a slight high pitched giggle that stopped her in her tracks. For a moment she couldn't be sure if what she had heard was in the room with her or not.

Suddenly acutely aware of her surroundings, she realized the pair of voices she heard had been coming from behind a large wall of hanging heavy winter coats.

Against her better judgment she slowly turned around.

It was obvious from the types of intimate-sounding noises and heavy breathing what kind of activities these *voices* were engaged in. Her natural instinct would normally have been to mind her own business and leave right then.

Tonight, however, her behaviour seemed to be contrary to anything normal.

Unable to stop herself, with her curiosity surprisingly piqued, she found herself slowly moving toward the coats. Unsure of what was drawing her closer she peered innocently through the mass of fur and wool.

It was a mere fraction of a second that she saw his face through the tiniest of spaces between two coats, but she knew in an instant that it was him. Without giving it a thought, she slowly separated the coats to verify her worst fear.

Still in the rapturous throws of passion, Brett and an unrecognizable waitress were intertwined in an intense embrace. They didn't even notice that someone else was in the room with them.

As she took in the images before her, the room began to spin and all noises became mute, as her mind subconsciously blocked as many details as possible. Completely bewildered, her knees began shaking and she wondered how she was still standing.

Looking up and instantly noticing the unmistakable look of shock and utter humiliation on her face, the young, embarrassed girl underneath Brett interrupted him and pointed sheepishly in Rebecca's direction.

As he reluctantly looked up at Rebecca, the look of sheer shock and shame on Brett's face was stunning. As if frozen in time for a moment, he said nothing and didn't appear to even be breathing.

Clearly realizing no words in the world would be heard in this moment, he didn't even attempt an explanation. There simply was nothing to say.

Rebecca's jaw dropped involuntarily and her heart plummeted in her chest. She impulsively covered her mouth with a shaking hand, unable to speak. In an instant, everything seemed to be moving in slow motion, and it was difficult to adequately comprehend what she saw.

Her previous mood instantly disintegrated, and several new emotions filled her at once, each of them equally painful.

Her immediate instinct was to run but her brain, not entirely able to communicate with her body at the moment, was overloaded with information. As she looked deeply into Brett's shameful eyes it took a concentrated effort to turn away from him. As her legs finally caught up with her racing mind, she literally bolted from the small room without looking back.

She had absolutely no idea where she was running to, other than *far* away from Brett. She raced down the long corridor as fast as allowable in heels and an evening gown, with Brett calling frantically after her, stumbling as he struggled to zip his pants.

Desperate to put some distance between them, she cringed just at hearing his voice. She couldn't bear to hear anything he had to say right now. He simply was not the person she thought he was.

Admittedly, she had always had an untarnished and clearly idealized image of Brett since the day they met. It honestly had never, ever occurred to her that he was even capable of something like this. Ironically, the very idea of causing Brett this exact pain and heartache was the one thing that had always stopped her from even considering being with Michael. Being that cruel went against every fibre of her being.

In the end she had chosen Brett.

Unfortunately she now felt extremely naïve thinking that he held their relationship to the same high standard. As she came to terms with this realization, the pain she felt from Brett's betrayal was shocking even to her. She was genuinely wounded by what he had just done, by what she had just witnessed, and she struggled to erase the image from her memory.

She truly believed Brett loved her and would not betray that love. She also realized her feelings for Brett had been much stronger than she had been willing to admit to herself all along. As much as she cared for Michael, she was willing to suppress those feelings and be faithful to Brett because ultimately she truly did love him.

In the midst of her newfound pain and heartbreak, she knew one thing for certain. She desperately wanted to be as far away from Brett and everyone else as humanly possible right now. Feeling completely humiliated and embarrassed, she knew her strength to hold everything together could only be possible in solitude.

She knew it was wrong and hurtful to skip out on Leo and Isabel's wedding like this but the thought of facing anyone, especially those so close to her and Brett would be too much to bear. With the wedding day mostly over, she had fulfilled her obligations as maid of honour for the most part, and figured that Leo and Isabel would certainly understand given the circumstances.

She cringed as she briefly considered the inevitable aftermath. Knowing how protective Leo had always been of her during her life she could only imagine what would be in store for Brett after tonight.

Desperately trying to refocus and organize her thoughts, she quickly decided to head back to their private suite for her things. She didn't know where she would go from there but knew that there was no possible way she could stay in that room with Brett now. Focusing on the fastest route she began making her way toward the guest quarters.

As she quickly turned a corner she abruptly collided head-on into someone walking toward her. Momentarily off balance, she refused to look up and lose her composure. She attempted to continue running without an exchange, but was stopped in her tracks by two sturdy hands holding her shoulders, anchoring her where she stood.

She knew instantly who had caught her.

"Rebecca, what's wrong? Are you okay?" Michael's soothing voice asked.

Out of breath, her body was as rigid as stone as she struggled for release, still refusing to look up at him or say a word. Making eye contact with Michael of all people in this moment of complete emotional upheaval would be catastrophic.

"Slow down, what happened?" he asked with a concerned tone, refusing to let go.

In the distance, Rebecca could vaguely hear Brett running down the hall after her.

"Please let me go, Michael. I have to go," she whispered in a panicked voice. "I'm sorry, I can't explain right now." She looked up briefly, pleading with her eyes.

Visibly concerned, he gently released her without a word as Brett approached.

Grateful for his compliance, Rebecca ran away as quickly as possible, thanking him under her breath as she left him. She truly wished she had the strength and the time to explain what had just happened but her main priority at the moment was to flee.

Regret filled her as she pictured the caring, worried expression on his face. For now she would simply have to push Michael from her thoughts and deal with the situation at hand.

Her immediate reaction to Brett's infidelity was almost instinctual in nature as if she had no other choice than to cut and run. Buried latent feelings and distant memories began to emerge as she ran. Unwilling to acknowledge these familiar painful emotions, she struggled to suppress them and refocus her mind.

The unequivocal feeling of déjà vu, however, was almost unshakable.

As she finally reached the room, her actions became somewhat mechanical in nature. Without a second thought she quickly gathered her belongings from the bathroom and bedroom and swiftly packed them in her suitcase. Oblivious to how ridiculous she looked, she changed into her snow boots, put her winter coat on over her dress, and headed toward the door. Anything she left behind didn't matter now.

As she reached for the door it opened suddenly, startling her.

Brett stood in the doorway looking dishevelled and out of breath. His expression was one of shame and regret and as he looked down at her suitcase, panicked confusion.

"What are you... Where are you going?"

"I'm leaving," she affirmed, more confidently than she thought possible.

"Rebecca... wait. Please," he pleaded, clearly unprepared for the approaching conversation. He awkwardly stepped inside the room as she stepped back in response.

As she looked at Brett now, trying to block the persistent images of him and the waitress in the coat room, she felt as if she was looking at someone completely unfamiliar to her. His very presence made her uncomfortable, which broke her heart.

"No, Brett. What could you *possibly* say to me at this point?"

She attempted to squeeze past him, heading for the door again. He stopped her by the arm more forcibly than intended.

"*Don't!*" she protested, glaring angrily at him. The audacity of his touch sent shivers down her spine. Looking at him now filled her with anger, pain, and disgust. Looking away, she could feel hot tears welling up in her eyes as her emotions soared out of her control.

He released her arm slowly, desperately trying to make eye contact, but she refused to look at him. She closed her eyes taking a deep breath to calm herself.

"I'm *so* sorry Rebecca. The last thing I wanted to do was hurt you. I know you probably don't believe me, but it's true."

As sincere as he sounded, she couldn't imagine how he could say this to her after what she had just seen. She was at a loss for words.

Becoming aware of the light-headedness from the adrenaline rush she was on, she found herself stumbling past him toward the door, struggling to steady herself.

Clearly concerned for her but careful not to touch her again, he reached out for her.

"Where are you going to go?"

"I don't know. I'll figure something out. I can't stay here with you."

Steeling herself, she opened the door not knowing where she would go next.

"Then you take the room and I'll go."

Obviously filled with regret, this was the only peace offering he could give.

# Behind the Glass

Although she did appreciate the offer, she was too proud and too stubborn to accept. As illogical as it was, she couldn't relinquish her right to leave *him* right now.

"No, thank you," she said, more coldly than intended. Despite his subsequent efforts, her anger was clearly closer to the surface than she realized.

Taking a deep breath, she walked out the door without looking back at him. Once in the hallway, Brett responded with something that instantly got her attention.

"Are you really *that* surprised by this, Rebecca?"

Stunned, she slowly turned around.

"I tried to make it work with you," he defended, "more than anyone I've ever been with. But you never... I don't know, let me in. You never wanted to take our relationship to the next level. I had hoped that you would want to move in together and I *tried* to be patient, but ..."

"You *tried*?!" she demanded. Another powerful rush of adrenaline filled her. "Don't you *dare* try to make this *my* fault. I would have *never* done this to you."

Based on Brett's expression, her sudden flash of anger spoke volumes to his pathetic attempt at a defence. Obviously not realizing what he had just implied, another blatant look of shame stared back at her.

Simply baffled by his excuses, the need to be as far away from him and this place was stronger than ever. At this point it would have been less hurtful if he had just let her go without an explanation. Amazingly he was making it worse.

There was nothing left to say to him and she refused to dignify the conversation with any further discussion. Emotionally she was beyond her limit. She turned and headed down the hall, away from him; away from his excuses and away from the pain he had caused her.

"No, I suppose you wouldn't have," Brett murmured as she left. She closed her eyes trying not to hear his last comment, focusing on finding a way home.

The grey-haired woman at the front desk was pleasantly distracted, looking out the window at the falling snow when Rebecca approached. The main lobby was peacefully quiet and virtually empty because of the wedding, which gave her a rare break to relax. Lost in thought, she barely noticed Rebecca approach the desk until she spoke.

"Excuse me," Rebecca interrupted softly, breaking the peaceful silence, "I was wondering if you could help me." Her voice was shaky and weak and tears covered her face.

Instantly noticing this, the woman behind the desk gave her a mothering, concerned look.

"Well, hello, dear. Are you alright?"

Grateful for her concern, she tried to compose herself enough to carry a normal conversation.

# Behind the Glass

"Yes... I'm fine. I was wondering if I could call a cab. I need to get home tonight."

Her voice was slowly getting stronger and she attempted to smile, but based on the woman's expression, she wasn't very convincing.

"Tonight, dear? Oh no, I'm afraid that won't be possible. With this storm, no one will be coming or going until the morning when we can clear everything out. The weatherman says the snow won't be letting up until at least after four. It looks like you'll have to wait. I'm sorry, honey."

She tried to soften the blow with kindness and a warm smile but the feeling of panic washing over Rebecca was overwhelming.

She was so distracted she hadn't even noticed the snow storm outside the walls that now held her captive. Frantically thinking of another solution to her dilemma, she asked the first thing that came to mind, "Can I get another room then, until the morning? Please?"

She didn't intend to sound so desperate but at this moment felt extremely helpless and trapped. If she couldn't escape, she would hide.

"I'm sorry, dear, but with all of the wedding guests this weekend, all of our rooms are completely booked." She reached her hand out to Rebecca. "Do you have a friend who might be willing to share a room with you for tonight?"

Unfortunately, she hadn't thought her plan through very carefully and was now left with few options. Feeling completely confounded she began considering alternative solutions, all of which were quite limited.

Had her mom been there with her this weekend as planned, she would have been the obvious choice, but she'd come down with the flu and stayed home.

The only two people she would have normally felt comfortable imposing upon in a situation such as this had just gotten married and were about to enjoy their wedding night together. Asking for their help wasn't even a remote option.

Brett *had* offered their room, but given her intensely negative feelings toward him right now, that was definitely not an option either.

The only other person she would even consider staying with was Claire. As this option crossed her mind, she pictured the inevitable drama that would ensue, not to mention Claire's need to talk incessantly and insensitively about every detail of the situation. Reliving Brett's infidelity and discussing it in detail – with Claire of all people – was an utterly unappealing option. Unfortunately it didn't look as if she would have a choice.

Discouraged, Rebecca thanked the woman for her help, telling her she would find a friend to stay with, and slowly made her way with her suitcase to a giant leather couch in front of an inviting, calming fireplace in the middle of the main lobby.

Still in her coat and bridesmaid gown, with smeared makeup on her face, she sat dazed and completely drained, gazing at the burning embers before her.

Reflecting on recent events, this evening certainly had not turned out the way she had envisioned. Any feelings of excitement or anticipation had been extinguished with dysphoria. Now, only an overpowering numbness began to set in.

Normally never one for self-pity, she was feeling extremely hurt and alone. She fought the paralyzing urge to cry with every fibre of her being. With her thoughts completely scattered, she wondered if she had somehow deserved this because of how she felt about Michael...

Her heart sank, and skipped a beat at the same time, as the mere thought of Michael crossed her mind for a brief moment. Memories of tonight became bittersweet as she recalled what they had shared that evening.

She wished she hadn't left him the way she did, wished she could have explained things to him in the hallway earlier, wished she could have taken photos of him all evening to remember him by, but most of all she wished she could be with him again, even if only to serve as a distraction from the unpleasant reality she was now facing.

Feeling helpless and despondent, she craved how she always felt in his presence. When she was with him she felt complete and confident. After what Brett had just put her through tonight, she needed to feel that way again, now more than ever.

On the verge of tears, she crossed her arms tightly, hugging herself as she focused on the beautiful dancing flames before her, secretly wishing he was there with her. Holding her.

After a few quiet moments, as if she had somehow beckoned him... *he was there.*

She had been so completely lost in her own thoughts, staring at the mesmerizing fire, that she hadn't even noticed he had been standing directly in front of her.

He seemed to appear virtually out of nowhere.

He looked down at her with warm, attentive eyes. His tie was missing and the first two buttons on his shirt were undone, giving him a more casual look. His face appeared flush, and his massive frame obscured the soft glow from the fireplace. As she looked back up at him her heart soared with a mix of emotions, yet she found it more difficult to hold back her tears. She didn't know what she would say to him now, even if she could find the ability to speak.

Without a word, he gently took her by the hand, picked up her suitcase, and slowly led her out of the main lobby. She couldn't be sure, but based on his body language he seemed to be completely aware of her situation, knew exactly what was going through her mind, and inexplicably, exactly what she needed.

She didn't argue or resist or even speak. She simply followed him, not knowing where he was taking her. The manner in which he led her was

# Behind the Glass

focused, and his grip on her hand was protectively firm.

In her bemused state as they continued down the long hallway, it finally occurred to her that he was rescuing her.

# CHAPTER SIX

*Safe*

If he had been prone to violence and less in control of his emotions, Michael probably would have punched Brett right then and there. At the very least, he would have given him a piece of his mind when he saw him in the hallway a few minutes ago. Instead he was far more concerned with what Brett's predictable infidelity had done to Rebecca. Grudgingly taking the high road, he simply gave Brett a disapproving glare and snapped, "You're unbelievable, man, you know that?" as Brett frantically raced by.

Michael now felt thoroughly foolish for believing that perhaps Rebecca had reformed Brett from his previous womanizing tendencies. Brett hadn't changed at all since their college days. As always, monogamy was simply *not* in his vocabulary.

Only, now Rebecca was the unfortunate collateral damage left behind.

Knowing the strong, and somewhat rare, moral code Rebecca lived by, Michael could only imagine what this had done to her. He had seen her anguish for himself in that brief moment in the hallway earlier. Her eyes, as always, spoke volumes.

The very idea of pain such as this overcoming her, made him cringe with an anger and helplessness he had never known. The need to be with her, to comfort her, to protect her was unprecedented. Consoling her became his only priority.

Patiently giving her the space she would need to deal with Brett, he made his way back to the reception hall to discretely inform Leo and Isabel that Rebecca was under the weather and would likely not be returning.

It was anyone's guess as to what excuse Brett would eventually give the bride and groom, and Michael wanted to give her the dignity and privacy she deserved.

After Brett finally had resurfaced, it wasn't difficult to find Rebecca. Knowing that she would likely be too angry to stay anywhere near Brett tonight, he hoped to find her in the main lobby looking for alternative accommodations.

To his genuine relief he found her.

Despite how stunningly beautiful she looked by the glowing light of the fireplace, she also appeared irrevocably damaged by Brett's inexcusable behaviour. As she gazed at the fireplace, deep in thought, it seemed as though every ounce of energy was being spent on maintaining her composure. Based on her intense expression, it wasn't surprising to find her completely unaware of Michael's presence as he approached.

As predicted, Brett's indiscretions had hit Rebecca hard, efficiently transforming her into an almost catatonic state. In such a cynical world, it was considerably rare to find an innocence and unconditional trust such as this. Sadly, that naïve part of her would be forever changed. He could see it in her eyes the moment he approached.

He could only hope the damage done tonight was not permanent. Right now, more than anything, she would need a friend. Someone neutral, someone *safe*.

As he led her by the hand to his guest suite he was thankful for her consent. The last thing he wanted to be right now was another form of stress in her evening. He simply wanted to give her a place to hide, to rest, and hopefully to heal.

Upon entering the room, he placed her suitcase in a corner and led her to a small couch. He carefully took her coat and replaced it with a crocheted blanket around her shoulders as she slowly sat down. Still clearly unwilling to attempt eye contact and utterly silent, she visibly fought back tears as she settled in.

Waiting patiently, he quietly sat in the armchair across from her as she eventually relaxed and regained emotional control. As far as he was concerned, he would wait all night if necessary, and do whatever was needed for her, even if that meant leaving her alone. He hoped she would feel comfort in his presence, but would understand if she wanted space.

# Behind the Glass

After several minutes, when he felt it was appropriate to break the silence, he spoke quietly, attempting to put her at ease.

"Rebecca," he began, "is there anything I can do for you? Anything you need?"

He looked at her with a kind and purposely platonic expression, hoping she would come out of her shell. It took a few moments for her to respond, but her mood lightened as she spoke.

"You've done so much for me already, probably more than you realize. I'm incredibly grateful. Thank you."

She finally looked at him with calmer, less troubled eyes. She seemed to be more at peace. Her hair and makeup were still surprisingly flawless. Tears had erased some of her eye liner and mascara, but her delicate beauty hadn't faded in the least.

"It was the least I could do for you. Seeing you like that... I'm just so sorry you had to go through..."

Rebecca interrupted him mid-sentence with a shaky voice.

"Can we talk about something else, anything else? Please?"

Her calm state quickly transformed into uneasiness.

Feeling momentarily regretful for his direct nature in her presence, he hoped he hadn't made an indelible mistake. He couldn't blame her for not wanting to relive it.

"Of course, I'm sorry. That was thoughtless," he apologized, "What would you like to talk about? Maybe something to get your mind off things?"

He couldn't imagine what she would want to talk about at a time like this, but offered anyway. Assuming she would probably want to be left alone, he was surprised and totally unprepared by her answer.

"Tell me about growing up on a horse farm. What was it like?"

She asked him as if it was perfectly normal for her to know this about him.

It took him a few moments to respond. Her unpredictable nature was something he would probably never get used to. Ironically, he wouldn't have it any other way.

The opportunity to share details of his life with her was pleasantly unexpected, which made him smile as he slowly recounted.

"Well, it was a lot of things. It was a unique experience. Growing up around horses and living on a ranch far away from everything was completely normal to me, and for the most part, pretty amazing. At times it was lonely and a lot of hard work, but ultimately it shaped me into who I am today. I actually appreciate how lucky I am to have had that experience, and to grow up with such a close, supportive family."

# Behind the Glass

Thankfully she appeared genuinely distracted and seemed to hang onto his every word. "Tell me about them," she mused, clearly interested.

"Well, for as long as I can remember, we've always been a close-knit family. I suppose it naturally comes with the territory when the family business is Vale Ranch."

Her eyes widened and a tiny smile emerged.

"Vale? Your last name is Vale? I know that place. It's a horseback riding summer camp out in the country. *That's* where you grew up?"

He wasn't entirely surprised she had heard of his family's business. It was actually somewhat well known in Madison, but based on her reaction, he felt a stronger sense of pride as he described it to her.

"Yes, my father and Uncle Luke inherited the Vale family ranch from my grandfather years ago, and have kept it running together their entire lives. It's primarily run as a camp, but we also rent stables and board horses. It's really a beautiful place with trails spanning two hundred fifty acres out into the country in Mazomanie. It's about forty minutes west of Madison."

Smiling, she recalled, "Yes, I know. I remember. You're right, it *is* a beautiful place."

The coincidences and connections between them never seemed to end.

"You've been there?"

She smiled contently, daydreaming briefly before she spoke.

"Yes I have, when I was in middle school. My parents sent me there for a weekend of horseback riding camp right before their divorce. I think it was their idea of a distraction for me, to soften the blow. I was *such* a sucker for horses at that age." As she paused momentarily, a melancholy expression crossed her face. "It worked. Even now it's still one of my fondest childhood memories. Taking care of a horse all by myself at that age, and going riding all weekend was pure heaven."

Sensing the bitter sweetness of the memory, he gave her a moment before he responded. Casually bringing up her parents' divorce tonight, of all nights, couldn't have been easy for her.

"You know, we actually still offer that same weekend package today," he continued. "It's always been one of our most popular, and hasn't changed much over the years. We now have a choice of enrichment classes, too."

Michael couldn't help but wonder what the chances were that they had somehow met when she had stayed at the ranch. Odds were that they hadn't even crossed paths, given the number of children and teenagers that came through the camp year round, but in this case anything was possible.

Given the number of coincidences they'd shared already and the fact that they both knew Leo, they seemed destined to meet. He wouldn't be surprised if she happened to be the girl he had a secret crush on once, on one of the summer camps.

# Behind the Glass

"Really? That would have been wonderful when I was younger. What kinds of enrichment classes?"

She couldn't have asked a better question.

"Well, besides the required instruction of complete horse care, there are a bunch of choices depending on what the child's interests are. Kids can now choose from sports, crafts, literature, drama, or a variety of art classes that I teach."

"*You* teach all of these classes?" she asked, somewhat in awe. "I thought you were a struggling artist," she teased.

"I don't teach all of them," he clarified, smiling. "We actually have several instructors who specialize in different fields, but besides the riding lessons and horse care, I teach all of the literature and art classes."

Based on her expression she seemed genuinely impressed.

"So in addition to creating brilliant art, you're also a teacher? That must be incredibly fulfilling," she baited, subtly searching for more information.

He found her sudden coyness charming.

"Yes it is, exceptionally fulfilling, actually. I feel like I'm doing what I'm meant to do in life, as clichéd as that sounds. I suppose I've always had an affinity for teaching the kids at the camp, and just naturally loved being around them. For most of my life being surrounded by young people was really all I knew, so it came easily to me. When my parents recognized my interest, they encouraged me to go to college to pursue a teaching degree. Of course they never imagined I would want to teach at the ranch. They figured I would eventually leave home and find a life elsewhere."

"Really? With such a close-knit family and a business you've been involved in your whole life, why would they assume that?"

"If you knew my father, you'd understand. He loves Vale Ranch deeply, but I don't truly know if he would have chosen this life for himself. His younger brother, Luke, was always the more committed of the two, but looked to his big brother for guidance and support when it came to making decisions and keeping things running smoothly. So, being the loyal son and brother that he is, my father graciously took the family business over when the time came. Of course falling in love with my mother had something to do with it too," he said smiling. "The point is, my parents wanted to give me the choice to do something else with my life. They didn't want Vale Ranch to define who I am."

"It doesn't sound like it does. You seem very driven. You know what you want in life, which is such a rare thing. I think it's wonderful you teach kids at a ranch out in the country."

She looked back at him with sincere, kind eyes.

He was genuinely thankful for her continued interest in his life, and for the opportunity to look into her beautiful eyes again. Still, a part of him secretly wished the purpose of this conversation didn't only serve as a distraction from something horrible. For now though, he would accept it and tell her whatever she wanted to know.

"Thank you. I will admit that in *that* area of my life it's pretty great, and I feel exceptionally lucky to do what I love every day." His tone was somewhat sombre.

She picked up on it immediately.

"Did you grow up on the ranch alone, or did you have siblings to keep you company? You mentioned it was lonely at times."

She leaned in slightly and her expression became subtly empathetic.

"My parents run the ranch with Uncle Luke and Aunt Felicia. They have a daughter, Grace, who is a year younger than me. She's been more like a sister than a cousin to me my whole life. Luckily we always had each other growing up."

"Does Grace still work at the ranch too?"

"No..." he paused for a moment before continuing. "She and her husband, Ethan, live in Madison. You've actually met them." He watched her face intently to see if she would connect the dots and put everything together.

She looked slightly puzzled at first and then smiled, shaking her head slowly.

"Grace and Ethan own Behind the Glass."

"Yes, they do."

He knew this information would not upset her, but it would certainly get her mind going as she recalled their first meeting.

"So, they're more than just *good friends,* then," she concluded, smiling.

"I didn't mean to mislead you. It was just an easier explanation at the time."

"I understand. I was a complete stranger then." She paused for a moment then tilted her head slightly as she spoke, "Or was I?"

A small furrow appeared at her brow as she tried to piece together the mystery.

"Earlier tonight you said you'd been waiting weeks to talk to me. Did Grace have anything to do with that?"

"You could say that," he sighed. "She's a hopeless romantic and when she sees an opportunity, especially where *I'm* concerned, there's really no stopping her."

He rolled his eyes subtly as he spoke.

"She told you about *me?*" she asked, completely dumbfounded.

"Not exactly, she would never be that obvious. She knows me well enough to know that I'm not a huge fan of being set up, regardless of the good intentions behind it."

Based on Rebecca's sympathetic expression, he could tell she completely related to that feeling, and imagined a similar scenario with Leo and Brett.

"So she was sly about it then?" she teased, finally getting more comfortable with the idea that their first meeting was long in the making.

"Yes, she was. She invited me to the bookstore one evening when she knew you'd be there too."

Thinking back to the first time he had laid eyes on her instantly stirred a multitude of emotions at once. For a moment he found it difficult to maintain his composure.

"But how did Grace know..."

"That I would notice you?"

She focused for a long moment and looked at him with curious eyes.

"Yes. Why *me*?" she asked slowly.

It was clear that despite how they had both connected instantly with one another, she was still completely confused as to why. Why would *he* want *her*? He truly wished he could tell her everything he felt about her at that very moment, but tonight was definitely *not* the time.

Instead, he explained delicately.

"Grace knows me. She knows me *extremely* well. She's an unmatched judge of character, and can read people like no one I've ever known. I can't explain it. She just knew. And she was right to have me come that night. As much as I resist her romanticism at times, I'm grateful to her."

As he looked into her eyes, he was acutely aware of the line he was extremely close to crossing. He struggled to keep the conversation at a safe distance, hoping he hadn't gone too far.

Based on her body language, Rebecca seemed to be aware of the precarious territory they were heading into as well, and subtly veered the conversation in a new direction.

"So, Grace didn't have an interest in working for the family business then?"

"No," he said smiling widely. "Grace and I differ greatly in that way. She loves our family and the ranch very much, but has always longed for a life outside of it. She has an unbelievably outgoing personality by nature, and has an unyielding need to explore and experience new things all the time. She's always been the adventurer of the family."

"And you were the one who had to keep her out of trouble?"

"Exactly," he said, rolling his eyes. "You wouldn't believe how much more trouble she would have gotten into without me. She and I didn't always have consistent supervision on the ranch, and she pushed the limits a lot. Thankfully, in high school her interest and love of books completely took over and served as the perfect distraction. She would read for hours at a time, losing herself entirely in the stories. She was able to live vicariously through the characters in her books, and visit new and interesting places in her mind. And it kept her out of trouble," he shot her a quick smile.

"So it seems fitting that she now owns a bookstore."

"After she met Ethan, who is so much like her in every way, everything just naturally fell into place. They have both poured so much hard work and love into that store, and they're excited to see it doing so well. She finally has the life in Madison she always wanted."

"You seem very proud of her."

"I am."

He was also secretly envious of her. Not only had she found the life she wanted, but she had also found her soul mate in Ethan. Michael had never believed in the idea of soul mates as Grace had – until he met Rebecca. Only now did he finally understand what Grace had been talking about all those years.

As he looked at Rebecca, she seemed completely at ease. Her overall demeanour was calm, relaxed, and almost happy. All of the tension, anger, and hurt in her eyes seemed to wash away with each passing moment they were together. He felt relieved and profoundly fulfilled that he was able to comfort her. As he struggled to ignore the persistent need to hold her in his arms, he wished he could do more for her.

"Thank you, Michael," she said softly, as if reading his mind. "You'll never know how much I appreciate this. All of it."

As she looked at him, her gratitude seemed to reflect her innocence and vulnerability in that brief moment. In the end, despite his efforts to console her tonight, she was still quite wounded and broken. Michael sadly realized he could only do so much for her, for *now* anyway.

"You're welcome, Rebecca. I'm glad I'm able to be here for you. You actually seem much better."

"I am, trust me."

"Let me know if you need anything else though, alright?"

"Thank you. I honestly can't think of anything more you could do. You've truly been wonderful to me."

She smiled sweetly and sighed deeply, as if trying to calm herself. It seemed the idea of Michael taking care of her in this way stirred emotions that she was not yet ready to deal with.

"I loved learning about your life and your family. You're extremely lucky to have had such a unique childhood with such a loving family. From what I remember, Vale Ranch is an amazing place."

"You should visit again someday. We'd love to have you," he offered, almost impulsively. He hoped he hadn't sounded too forward.

"I would love to, actually. The opportunity to add images of horses and children and that majestic countryside to my portfolio would be incredible."

This caught Michael somewhat off guard.

"Your portfolio?"

"Oh. Yes. I'm a photographer, or at least I hope to be one day. I work for the *Isthmus* as a staff photographer right now, but I've slowly been putting together a portfolio of my work to display at a gallery one day." She looked as if she'd given away a big secret. "That's my plan anyway."

He was genuinely intrigued to learn this about her, and felt an immediate kinship with a newfound fellow artist. No wonder she connected to art the way she had that first night. Things were finally falling into place as more connections between them were being made.

"Wow, I had no idea. I'd really love to see your work sometime. Do you shoot in black and white or colour?"

Visibly excited at his interest, she relaxed immediately.

"Mainly black and white, although I dabble in colour occasionally. I find the creative process with black and white images so much more artistic. It's like moulding clay. You can manipulate it into a myriad of shapes. Black and white images can be strong, high contrast, and powerful, or they can be so soft, gentle, and subtle. I also find it extremely therapeutic to develop the prints myself in a darkroom, and frankly, I think black and white photography can be so much more dramatic, and raw as art."

Seeing her completely passionate about art, as she had been that first night, was wonderfully inspiring. Despite anything negative she was feeling tonight, she could instantly get caught up in discussing photography and art endlessly.

"Have you considered displaying your work in the bookstore?"

It was an obvious question, but he wanted to know her answer.

She paused momentarily and blushed slightly.

"Honestly, I haven't had the nerve yet. I don't know if I'm ready, or if my work is even worthy at this point. I've been considering it for months."

"You should do it."

"You haven't even seen my work. How do you know...?"

"That it's good? I don't. But you really seem to *know* and understand art. You have a unique eye for it. I could see that a mile away the first night I saw you. You also have a passion for it. You don't realize how rare that is, and how few struggling artists truly have it. Besides, what have you got to lose?" He smiled, hoping to boost her confidence.

She seemed slightly overwhelmed at his enthusiasm, and shook her head, smiling in response. She clearly wasn't used to this type of support for her artwork.

"I don't know. Nothing I guess, only my pride. I'm a bit of a perfectionist when it comes to my own work. I'm probably overly critical."

"You don't say?" he teased. "Most artists are typically their own worst critics, but that's a *good* thing. High standards and constantly pushing yourself to do better is what makes incredible art." He paused momentarily and looked directly into her eyes. "Promise me right now that you'll do it."

Appearing somewhat caught off guard, she stared back at him with a perplexed expression before she spoke. "Seriously?" she asked with a tilted head and a smile.

"Seriously. Don't be afraid. Take the first step. You can do it," he assured her.

The irony of the advice he was now giving her about her artwork was surreal. He wondered if she would eventually catch on to the subtle double meaning.

"You can be very persuasive when you want to be, you know that?" She took a deep breath, smiling. "I suppose I'm running out of excuses..."

"I could mention it to Grace sometime," he politely offered.

"No. Thank you," she interrupted quickly, appearing to surprise even herself. "If I'm going to jump off the ledge, I have to do it on my own terms. I appreciate the offer, though."

"It may feel like jumping off a ledge but you won't fall, you'll fly. Trust me."

Based on her demeanour, this particular boost to her ego seemed to be exactly what she desperately needed at this moment. Not only did it get her mind off of tonight's unfortunate events, but it refocused her thoughts on what she loved the most and on her future. For the first time tonight she seemed truly unburdened and completely relaxed. He hoped this feeling would last at least until the morning. She had suffered enough in the last few hours and deserved some peace.

She smiled widely for the first time tonight, which was a breath-taking sight, and agreed.

"Okay, you've convinced me. I'll do it, I will. I don't know why it's been so difficult to consider taking a risk with my work. Photography has always been such a passion of mine, but a part of me has always only considered it *just* a hobby." She looked deeply into his eyes. "Thanks for giving me the extra push I clearly needed."

"My pleasure, you just needed to hear it from someone who's been there and knows what it feels like to take that particular risk. Ultimately it's not easy to let yourself, your artwork, be vulnerable and exposed for the world to see. But when you see that *one person* truly connecting with what you are expressing as an artist, it makes it all worth it in the end."

Their eyes locked for a long moment as the atmosphere gradually became more serious.

She looked back at him with beautiful, tender eyes.

"Speaking from personal experience?" she asked, clearly knowing the answer.

"Yes. It's a moment that stays with you. A moment you'll never forget."

And the moment he knew he *had* to know her.

"And do you know for certain that person understands the feelings you are trying to provoke with your art?"

"Based on the person's facial expression, you have a pretty good idea. You can see it in their eyes, especially if you're looking for it."

# Behind the Glass

He could sense the hypothetical portion of the conversation was quickly fading. That same line he knew shouldn't be crossed tonight was clearly in sight as she looked back at him with a familiar look of longing. Earlier he may very well have acted on his feelings for her, but after what had transpired this evening, and how emotionally vulnerable she was probably feeling, he simply would not allow himself to make that mistake. As much as it pained him to end this flirtatious volley, his moral compass was stronger than his desire.

He smiled and looked down momentarily to break the sensitive tension.

"I suppose it also helps to interrogate that person after they've connected with your artwork, but not reveal you're the artist. Of course this is just a random theory," she teased, clearly attempting to change the tone of the conversation as well.

Surprised by her unexpected sarcasm, Michael laughed.

"Okay, you've got me there. I'll admit that it's not the recommended method to elicit feedback, but I stand by it, and would do it again in a second."

She smiled at his equally sarcastic response.

"I'm glad you did."

As they shared a few moments of comfortable silence, Michael was grateful for this time together with her. Despite the unfortunate reasons for their paths crossing in this particular way, they were able to learn things about one another and reach a comfort zone they hadn't had before tonight – friendship. Considering what Michael had originally anticipated for this weekend, he was thankful for this unexpected gift.

As Rebecca relaxed, sinking slowly into the plush couch, it was becoming apparent how truly exhausted and emotionally drained she was. Her demeanour was calm and serene, yet her eyes were heavy as she subtly yawned. Michael assumed that it had been a long day for her, even before tonight's dramatic conclusion, and decided to suggest that she get some much needed rest, despite not wanting this time with her to end.

"Well, it's been a long day, and I imagine you'd like to get some sleep. You're welcome to take the bed, and I'll take the couch. I can step out for a few minutes to give you some privacy if you'd like."

He chose his words carefully and was doing his best to make her feel comfortable.

"Thank you, Michael. You have no idea how much I appreciate all of this. I'm in your debt."

Tonight he would have done anything for her, without expecting a thing in return. It was nice however, to know she felt this way.

"I'm just glad I was able to give you a place to *hide out* for a while," he said with a playful smile.

As always, he instantly put her at ease. She smiled widely and shook her head as she giggled quietly. Obviously she understood the irony as well.

# Behind the Glass

Without another word, Michael quietly stepped out and took a short stroll through the hotel. With the reception over, few guests were even awake, much less wandering the halls, so he luckily didn't encounter anyone who would be asking about his or Rebecca's whereabouts this evening. As he walked, he wondered if their absence had affected Leo and Isabel's evening at all, and hoped their obvious bliss overshadowed anything negative tonight.

After an appropriate amount of time, he returned to the suite to find Rebecca settled in the bed with only a single lamp illuminated next to the door. The light was dim, and it was somewhat difficult to make out her face clearly from across the room, but as his eyes slowly adjusted to the light, she looked like an angel. She seemed to already be fast asleep and appeared utterly peaceful.

After making himself comfortable on the adjacent couch, he lay awake for hours, simply watching her sleep and recalling tonight's conversation. As he admired her exquisite beauty, he again memorized every curve, every line, every delicate detail of her beautiful face. For him this was the only face he would ever want to see at the end of every day... for the rest of his life.

Filled with an indescribable sense of peace, he was unequivocally sure.

She would need time to heal. He knew that. But now at least there was a chance, a possibility of something more. And he would wait for as long as she needed.

# CHAPTER SEVEN

*Friends*

As Rebecca hung up the phone, she hoped she had sounded convincing enough for her mother this time. She hated worrying her like this. It was the fourth call this week.

In reality, she wasn't being *completely* dishonest when her mom had asked how she was 'holding up' since Brett 'broke her heart.' Truthfully, she wasn't entirely 'fine,' as she had told her mom, but she definitely wasn't herself yet either.

At this point, Brett hadn't actually been on her mind as much anymore. Yes, his infidelity had hurt her, and it had taken time to come to terms with what he had done to her, but that wasn't the sole reason she had become an intentional shut-in for the past few weeks. That unfortunate incident seemed to only open the door to so much more.

Throughout most of Rebecca's life she had learned to systematically block the painful memories of her childhood. Putting up walls and compartmentalizing feelings of the past had become second nature. Over the years and into adulthood, she had become an expert at protecting herself with a thick skin while denying her true feelings. It was like breathing.

As she picked up the family photo album she had looked through so many times over the past few weeks, she closed her eyes, took a long cleansing breath, and finally allowed herself to reach deep into her psyche and remember. Letting the memories flood her mind was something she had resisted for years, but as she had recently come to realize, something necessary to move forward.

As painful as it was.

She was eleven years old when her parents divorced. Until then, she remembered her parents having a seemingly perfect marriage, and by extension, a perfect family. Rebecca and her younger brother, Trey, had by all accounts a fairly typical, happy childhood. Their father, Thomas Jordan, was a general surgeon at a local practice on the east side of town, and their mother, Madeline, was a nurse at St. Mary's Hospital downtown. They had been together since college and had always appeared incredibly in love. Their schedules were hectic at times, but they both always managed to make time for their family. They vacationed to Door County in the summers, and spent holidays together in their home.

As normal and happy as their life seemed to be, it was merely an illusion.

In her parents' defence, they had made their best effort to hide their imperfections from their impressionable young children, but despite their

# Behind the Glass

good intentions, Rebecca eventually put the pieces of the story together on her own. Unfortunately, adults don't always realize how much kids absorb, especially at age eleven.

At first, Dr. Jordan's absences and late nights seemed completely normal. His practice was growing and it gradually required more and more of his time. Business was good and the success of it was exciting. Slowly over time, the cancelled lunch dates, the missed dinners, soccer games, and dance recitals filled Madeline with doubt. Doubt inevitably lead to suspicion, and eventually, distrust and an unyielding curiosity.

From what Rebecca had been able to decipher over the years, *it* had happened on a cold November day when her mother's intuition finally got the best of her. Hoping her imagination was running wild, she decided to confront her worst fears directly by paying her husband of fifteen years a visit at his office during his lunch hour. She found him in an extremely compromising position with one of the nurses in his private office.

The details of the aftermath had been lost over the years, but based on her mother's private grief, were unbearable.

Unfortunately, this was not the worst part.

A year later, Rebecca's parents were divorced, she and her brother were living with their mother, and their father was remarried... with a new baby.

To say Rebecca's world was turned upside down during that year was a vast understatement. It changed Rebecca in ways she would realize for years to come.

The development of a strict moral code that would guide her decisions throughout her life started early. Sheltering her baby brother, three years her junior, and having to endure her family breaking apart, had quickly transformed her from a carefree child into a responsible adolescent.

Madeline, taking the high road as she always had, did her best to make the whole ordeal easier on the children. She never once uttered a negative word about their father in front of them, and was extremely private with her true emotions. She handled the scandal of her marriage with grace and great strength, and simply carried on with life. She continued working as a nurse while raising two children on her own and never asked their father for a thing.

Thankfully, she and her children were steadily supported by a close knit group of friends that included the Prescott family. A close bond that would continue for years to come was forged during that time, for which Rebecca was always grateful.

Rebecca and Trey visited their father on the weekends and certain holidays, but their relationships with him were never the same. He had a new family and different priorities, and didn't always balance everything as well as he could have.

# Behind the Glass

Initially Rebecca thought she would never forgive her father, but over the years as she matured into an adult who made her own mistakes, she gradually let go of most of the negative feelings she harboured toward him. These days she didn't have a particularly close relationship with him and he had simply become a neutral force in her life. Like her mother, she continued living her life and never asked her father for a thing, monetarily or otherwise.

What she didn't fully realize until quite recently was how his actions had shaped her ideas and expectations of relationships and ultimately, of men.

Spending night after night analysing what went wrong with Brett brought her to a conclusion that she had been afraid to face. As hard as it was to admit, on a certain level she expected Brett to hurt her if she let herself become vulnerable. Ironically, she had been so busy protecting herself – putting up familiar walls – that she failed to see the damage it ultimately did to their relationship. In the end, he hurt her anyway.

With this, she finally realized her dilemma. How could she open herself to love again without getting hurt? This had been the question invading her thoughts and eluding her for the past several weeks. The only conclusion she could make at this point was that she wasn't good for anyone right now.

Despite her sombre state of mind, the weeks of solidarity and self-analysis had actually proved extremely productive. Rebecca was able to throw herself into the one thing that not only served as a much needed form of therapy, but had always been something she truly loved and had given her great joy – her photography.

Keeping the promise she made to Michael, and after spending endless hours in her dark room, she was finally able to refine and perfect a select collection of her artwork to submit to Behind the Glass.

Ironically, jumping off the ledge was easier than she had ever imagined.

The initial meeting to present her portfolio to Grace and Ethan was surprisingly relaxed and somewhat anticlimactic. She couldn't help but feel a little foolish for getting so worked up about sharing her art with others.

They were kind, down-to-earth people who were so easy to talk to, and their immediate response to her art was extremely positive. After a somewhat informal presentation of what she believed to be her best work, they discussed their selection process and told her she'd hear from them in a couple weeks.

Every month the shop consulted with a group of local artists whom Ethan networked with throughout the years, and who helped decide if the art was worthy of displaying in the store. In some cases, the art could potentially be submitted elsewhere later, such as other art galleries or local art museums. This could end up being a huge stepping stone to becoming a bona fide photographer.

# Behind the Glass

As excited as she was to finally take the first step as a struggling artist, deep down she knew she had only one person to thank for it. Other than her family, she had never had the support she needed to feel confident about her photography. Brett had unintentionally belittled it during their relationship, making her feel as if it were just a pipe dream. Michael, on the other hand, had filled her with inspiration and made her believe in herself again.

Inexplicably, he had the ability to connect with her in a way no one had before.

It was this connection that confirmed once again what she had known in her heart to be true since the night they had met. Simply put, he was *the one*, her soul mate, and she had never before had such strong feelings for anyone in her life.

Ironically, it was these feelings that fuelled her aversion to taking a chance on love. As much as she truly wanted to love again, to let go of her fears and allow herself to be vulnerable, the idea of losing Michael was unbearable. It could potentially destroy her. Forever.

So in the interest of self-preservation, she decided that keeping him at a safe distance seemed to be her only alternative until she made peace with her mind-boggling dilemma. Putting herself in a position of getting hurt again was simply not an option right now.

Despite the momentary urges to talk to him again, she resisted answering the phone twice in the last couple of weeks when he called.

His tone was delicate yet genuinely concerned:

*"Hi Rebecca, it's Michael. I imagine you don't really feel like talking right now, but I wanted to check in on you anyway, and let you know that I'm thinking about you, and hope you're doing okay. If you ever need a friend to talk to, I'm here. Call me anytime... Take care of yourself, Rebecca."*

Late one night when she was feeling her absolute lowest, repeatedly replaying the coatroom scene in her mind, and allowing herself to feel the pain while having a good therapeutic cry, Rebecca played Michael's message over and over again until she had it memorized. Hearing the sincerity and care in his voice gave her more comfort than he would ever know, and it managed to get her through many sleepless nights. For that, she was eternally grateful.

Still, she wasn't ready to face him.

It was in these moments that the regret of not capturing him on film was the greatest. She closed her eyes and held onto the memory of him with every fibre of her being.

She would always remember how wonderful he had been to her that night. The simple act of talking to him and having him *really* listen to her brought her back from such a heartbroken place and gave her the strength and confidence she so desperately needed. She couldn't explain why, but being herself was completely effortless with him. She felt unconditionally accepted in a way she never had before.

As she sat on her couch with her eyes closed, holding her family photo album tightly to her chest, remembering every wonderful moment with him, the telephone suddenly rang, making her jump and breaking the peaceful silence.

Reluctantly, she opened her eyes and returned to reality.

Assuming it was most likely her mom again, not having been convinced by her earlier performance of normalcy, she answered it without hesitation.

To her sheer surprise, it was *not* her mother.

As she sat utterly speechless on the telephone, the voice on the other end repeated her name, hoping she was still there.

"Hello... Rebecca? Are you there?" the voice asked.

Finally, after eventually finding her own voice, she answered.

"Yes, I'm here," she said softly as a tiny smile reached her lips.

Her heart rate instantly doubled.

"It's Michael. How are you?"

He had the same concerned tone as before. Hearing his voice instantly filled her with a familiar feeling of utter peace.

"I'm," she hesitated, choosing to answer honestly, "getting better every day. Thank you for asking. How are you?"

"I'm good. I hope I'm not calling at a bad time. Leo gave me your phone number."

As always, he was a perfect gentleman.

A slight feeling of guilt rose to the surface as she spoke.

"I'm sorry I never returned your calls. I haven't been all that social lately. I appreciated it though. It really meant a lot to me." Probably more than he would ever know.

"I'm glad. And I understand wanting to be alone for a while. You needed time and space to process everything. I can only imagine."

For a brief moment, for the first time, she sensed true anger in his voice. It reminded her of how protective he was of her that night after the wedding. What Brett had done to her had clearly upset him more than she realized.

"Thank you."

She was unexpectedly grateful for how much he cared.

"Do you have any plans today?"

It was Sunday. She didn't have to work. She had no plans, but didn't particularly want to go anywhere or see anyone. Solidarity had become oddly comforting lately.

"Not really, why do you ask?"

"I have something I want to show you, something that might lift your spirits. Will you let me do that?"

# Behind the Glass

His familiar tone with her was refreshing. It made her smile for the first time in days. As much as she told herself to resist, she couldn't help herself.

"Sure, that would be nice. When?"

"Look out your window."

Her heart skipped a beat, and a sudden rush of excitement filled her as she hurried to the window. As she carefully peeked through her curtains to confirm he was outside, she almost forgot he was still on the other end of the phone as she lightly caught her breath at seeing his face again. She couldn't believe he was really here, right now.

"You're here? How did you..."

"Leo gave me your address. I hope you don't mind me showing up like this. I wasn't sure if you'd answer your phone or if you'd even be home, but I had to try. Is that okay?"

*It shouldn't be okay,* she thought. *He shouldn't be here right now.* She was supposed to be keeping her distance. She was, for lack of a better description, a complete mess right now, both emotionally and physically. She hadn't even gotten dressed yet today and was still in her robe and pyjamas, a fact she was now acutely aware of.

Panic began to build.

"Yes, it's okay... but you'll have to give me a few minutes to put myself together." She cringed immediately at the words she chose, unintentionally implying she was broken. "I just have to get dressed."

She was suddenly a ball of nerves.

"Of course, take your time. I'll be waiting outside, whenever you're ready."

He smiled in the direction of the window she was peering through.

After they hung up she lingered at the window for a few moments, admiring him. He was as handsome as ever, dressed casually in jeans, t-shirt, and a black jacket, leaning on his rugged black truck in the afternoon sunlight of a beautiful spring day. It was times like these that made her wonder what she had done to deserve the admiration of someone so out of her league.

As she dressed, scrambling to find something suitable to wear, she caught her reflection in the mirror. She stopped, took a long look at herself and wondered if he would see how the past several weeks had changed her. Although she wasn't the same person he had met in the bookstore café three months ago, she hoped her weeks of reflection had transformed her in a positive way.

Much like artwork on a canvas, she was undeniably a work in progress.

After she quickly washed her face, applied a touch of makeup to her lips and lashes, and combed her long lush caramel locks, she took a deep breath and opened the front door.

He smiled widely the instant he saw her. She was struck by his smile, how genuine it was, and how warm and inviting his body language had always been towards her. His dark hair was shorter, and he was clean shaven. To her delight, his clean-cut look made him even more handsome. Gazing at her with same beautiful eyes she had pictured in her mind these past weeks, he paused for a moment before he spoke.

"Hi there," he said as he approached her. "You look... perfect."

Clearly he had been longing to see her too.

"I don't know if I'd go that far but thank you. Would you like to come in?"

She had spent the previous day cleaning to keep her mind occupied so her home was actually quite presentable.

"Actually, what I have to show you isn't here. I have to take you to it. You might want to grab your jacket."

"Where are we going?" she asked as she reached for her favourite grey fleece next to the door. Without hesitation, Michael reached for it and helped her put it on.

"You'll see."

After she locked the door behind her he gently took her hand.

It was incredibly easy to just go with the flow with him. As he led her to his truck, she followed with wonder, trusting him completely.

"You're not even going to give me a hint?"

She already knew the answer.

"Trust me, you won't be disappointed. Besides, where would the fun be in that?"

She sensed he was enjoying doing this for her so she went with it.

As they approached his massive black truck, he opened the door for her and she stepped inside. It was a simple act, something that clearly came naturally to him, but at this moment it made her feel thoroughly taken care of. And it wasn't the first time she felt this way with him.

Throughout most of her life she had always been the caregiver: to her brother, to her friends, even at times to her mother. With him, she didn't feel this way.

Smiling again, she relaxed as they drove off.

"Leo says hello, by the way. He's been really worried about you."

That was an understatement. After their honeymoon, Rebecca broke the news to Leo and Isabel as delicately as possible, but it didn't matter. Leo not only partially blamed himself for what had happened with Brett, but confronted him in the days that followed, warning him to stay the hell away from Rebecca. Predictably, Brett complied without argument. He knew he had crossed a line and there was no going back.

"I know," she said sadly, "I've been talking to him and Isabel every few days lately. It's not his fault, but he feels responsible. He keeps saying he should have seen it coming, which I don't understand."

Michael gave her a quick, concerned glance.

"He's just extremely protective of you. He feels he made a big mistake setting you up with Brett. He hates seeing you hurting like this. I can't say I blame him."

"I know, and I appreciate that, but he has to realize he can't protect me from everything. I went into this with my eyes open. No one forced me to be with him. How could Leo possibly know this would happen? It's not his fault."

She looked out the window thinking of Leo and how he had always been there for her. During the divorce, during every milestone of her life, he had always looked out for her. She wished she could convince him not to blame himself for this.

"It's Brett's fault," she finally said.

She may have pushed him away, but Brett was responsible for his own actions. She would not allow herself or anyone else to take the blame for what he'd done.

"You look like you're holding up alright, though." Sensing tension in her voice, Michael changed the subject. "I think what I have to show you will be exactly what you need today."

The instant they made eye contact she felt better.

"You definitely have me wondering," she admitted, looking out the window in wonder.

They were heading downtown, which unfortunately didn't narrow the possibilities much. She couldn't even guess where he was taking her.

"So, how have you been doing? How are things at the ranch?"

As she glanced over, quickly admiring him as they drove, she realized how much she had missed talking with him, knowing about his life.

"I've been good. It's the slower season right now, so it's given me some time to get back to doing what I love most."

"Which is?"

"Painting. It always feels good to get back into the studio."

She could relate to this idea completely. Her darkroom had become her oasis.

"I know the feeling."

"So you've been back in the darkroom?"

"Yes. I'm surprised you didn't know. I guess Grace didn't mention it?"

She assumed Michael would have known and wondered why Grace had kept quiet.

"Mention what?"

"I kept my promise," she began, trying to contain her excitement. "I finally submitted my work to Behind the Glass. I'm just waiting to hear back from them."

"That's awesome, Rebecca! I'm so glad to hear you finally did it. How did it go?"

He seemed genuinely surprised, which threw her. Maybe Grace didn't want Michael to hear the good news from anyone but her. It seemed fitting.

# Behind the Glass

He looked at her with warm eyes and she could feel his excitement. She instantly began to beam with a pride she only felt with him.

"You were right. It was easier than I thought it would be. Don't get me wrong, I'm still a bit of a nervous wreck, but it felt good to take the first step."

She couldn't explain it, but it felt right being with him at this moment. In the past few weeks, and throughout most of her life, she felt most comfortable doing everything on her own, always fiercely independent, but now it was refreshing having a *friend* to confide in. Sharing this news with him was exactly what she needed.

"It may not feel like it now, but that first step, putting your work out there for the world to see, is the biggest hurdle. It only gets easier from here. I promise," he said as he parked the truck at a metered parking spot downtown.

Rebecca had barely been paying attention to where they were going but based on the few landmarks she remembered passing, deducted that they were on a side street off of State Street. Considering State Street ran eight blocks from the State Capitol to the University of Wisconsin's campus, it was anyone's guess which one. Her sense of direction had admittedly gotten turned around. Being with Michael had that effect on her.

"Okay, we're here, but I need you to do something for me."

"Um, okay, what do you need me to do?"

"Close your eyes and keep them closed until I tell you to open them." He got out and walked to her side of the truck, opened the door for her, and held out his hand. "Trust me."

Something in his eyes reminded her of the first night they met when he had held her bookmark out to her. That kind smirk, that raised eyebrow... yes, she trusted him.

"Of course," she said softly as she closed her eyes, smiling.

As he led her by the hand down State Street, she tried to pinpoint where they were based on the noises she heard but nothing gave their location away. The street was crowded with voices: fragments of conversations passed by, children laughed in the distance, and music played from inside stores as doors opened and closed. Delicious aromas from restaurants filled the air but nothing specific triggered any clues as to where they were.

It was actually an exhilarating sensation being led blindly through the streets of Madison.

Her imagination began to wander as she speculated where he was taking her. She searched her memory, trying to remember which movies were in the theatres, which exhibits were being displayed at the local museums, what theatre production was being shown at the Civic Center, but for the life of her, she drew a complete blank.

The only clue she had was that he wanted to *lift her spirits.*

# Behind the Glass

Finally after about a block they stopped walking. He gently positioned her ninety degrees to the right and stood directly behind her. He placed both hands on her shoulders pulling her closer to him as he spoke softly into one ear, "You can open your eyes now."

As she opened her eyes, what stood before her almost took her breath away.

They were facing Behind the Glass, and in its windows were *her* black and white photographs glowing in the gallery light for all of State Street to see.

"I told you you'd fly," he whispered.

Seeing her artwork on display filled her with a pride and excitement she never knew possible. It was the happiest she'd felt in weeks.

"Oh my God... Michael, I... I'm speechless."

She leaned back into him in awe of what she saw before her. He wrapped his arms around her loosely as they stood together in front of the shop, taking in the moment.

Being in his arms and sharing this experience together felt so natural, so normal. The more she leaned into him, the tighter he held her. Feeling completely content, she closed her eyes for a few seconds, smiling. For one moment in time, everything was perfect, and she wished this feeling could last forever.

He gently released her and took her hand again.

"There's more inside. Grace and Ethan are waiting for us. Are you ready?"

She turned to face him but found it difficult to express her gratitude after their eyes met. Looking into his gorgeous eyes made her heart race as it had the first time she saw him.

"This is amazing. I'm just... overwhelmed. Thank you."

"You're welcome. I'm glad it made you happy but *you* deserve the credit. You did this on your own. You have so much talent and your work is breathtaking. I simply brought you here."

That was an understatement.

"No Michael, you've done so much more for me than that. I wouldn't be standing here looking at my photographs in these windows without your help, without *you*."

He looked at her, marvelling at the joy in her eyes, and didn't say a word. He squeezed her hand lightly and held it to his chest for a moment before leading her to the front door of the shop. As he opened the door for her, she saw Grace and Ethan waiting for them. They seemed to be as excited as she was. Grace hurried over and gave her a quick tight hug.

"Hi, Rebecca! Welcome to your first official gallery opening! What do you think?"

Grace gave Michael a quick glance and smiled proudly.

# Behind the Glass

"Hi Grace! Honestly, I think I'm still in shock. It hasn't really sunk in yet, but it's pretty amazing." Everything felt so surreal right now.

"Well, I can't tell you how hard it was *not* to call you and tell you, but Michael really wanted to do this for you." She smiled widely, clearly happy to see them here together again.

"I'm glad he did," Rebecca said as she turned to meet his eyes. "It's exactly what I needed today."

Almost unaware that he was still holding her hand, Michael gave it another light squeeze and smiled. Her heart skipped a beat.

"Well, your work is absolutely beautiful, my dear! We are so proud to have it displayed on our walls. You should be very proud too. It's gotten a lot of praise already."

She gave Ethan a quick glance, raising her brow.

"A good friend of mine owns a fine art gallery on Monroe Street called Mystic Art," Ethan explained. "We had lunch together last week and I showed him one of your photos. He's quite impressed and was surprised to hear this was your first show. He's coming by next week to view the rest of your collection to see if it's a good fit for his gallery. No promises, but this would be *huge* for you."

Rebecca couldn't believe her ears. This was so much more than she had ever expected. She had always had a passion for art and photography, and had learned as much as possible without much formal training, but had no idea she had this much natural talent. Obviously pouring her heart and soul into her art these last weeks had created something special. Michael had given her the push, but clearly she had done the rest on her own, as he'd said.

She couldn't help but beam with pride as she gazed around the shop.

"Wow, I don't know what to say. Thank you both so much for everything you've done for me. I think I'm still slightly stunned. This is a lot to take in."

It was something she had waited such a long time for and it was finally happening. She was finding it difficult to express how extraordinary it felt.

"I can only imagine," Grace said as she gave Rebecca's arm a light squeeze. "Feel free to browse around the shop at your work. It's pretty slow today so you'll have some privacy. Let me know if I can get you anything."

"Thanks, Grace." Rebecca was still glowing, gradually taking everything in.

Grace signalled to Ethan, and they both meandered to the rear of the shop. Grace glanced back at the two of them for a moment and smiled happily, forever the romantic.

Rebecca turned to Michael, who had been quietly listening, watching her enjoy the experience.

"Would you like to take a walk with me?"

"I don't think there's anything I'd rather do right now."

He led her by the hand to the wall opposite the main stair, where most of her work was displayed.

# Behind the Glass

They spent over an hour admiring her collection together, discussing what Michael saw in each photograph in comparison to what she had tried to capture on film. It was fascinating to examine art from both perspectives, and they clearly enjoyed getting caught up in it together.

Grace subtly watched them, pleased to see their happiness together as they laughed.

As they slowly headed up the stairs together, surveying her artwork, Michael lightly placed his hand on the small of her back as he followed slightly behind her. Every movement they made together seemed so natural with a comfortable familiarity.

Rebecca hadn't been this happy in a long while, probably ever, and she owed it all to this place, her cherished oasis. If she hadn't come here every week to escape she would have never met Michael. Some things, she decided were just meant to happen.

Later as they drove home together, Rebecca couldn't seem to stop smiling. It had been an unexpectedly wonderful day and everything was finally sinking in.

She had been in such a low place these last few weeks, but it all slowly faded away with each passing minute she spent with Michael. He made her feel good about herself and gave her the confidence she needed to move forward with her life.

"It's nice to see you so happy."

"It's been a long time... but yes, I *am* happy. Thank you so much for today. You always seem to know exactly what I need."

"Well, I was extremely motivated. Spending the day with you was something I've been looking forward to for a while."

She agreed and realized how much she had missed him too.

"It *was* an awesome day. I'm so glad you were with me."

"You'll never forget your first big break as an artist. Seeing your face light up today at the shop brought back a lot of memories. I'm glad I was there."

As he parked the truck in front of her house, she secretly wished their time together didn't have to end. She knew she wasn't remotely ready for anything more than friendship right now, but the need to spend more time with him was powerful.

"So I imagine going to work at the *Isthmus* tomorrow as a *showcased* photographer will feel different. Hopefully they appreciate the talent they have working for them," he teased as he got out of the truck. She found his sense of humour amusing.

As he opened her door and helped her out of the truck, she realized how much she enjoyed how he constantly looked after her. She was slowly getting used to it.

"Actually, I probably wouldn't be the photographer I am today without that job. I'll always appreciate how challenging it is making the ordinary extraordinary. It's honestly been the best education I could have asked for."

"I can imagine." He smiled as if recalling his own experiences as an artist. "I've always believed that practical experience in life is sometimes more beneficial than formal education. It's important to get your hands dirty."

"Learning by doing versus learning by thinking?"

They seemed to be completely in sync with each other.

"Something like that. Although there's something to be said for having an education too."

He raised one eyebrow, wondering if she'd picked up on the irony.

"Said the Art and Literature teacher," she smiled playfully.

"I wouldn't want to sound too hypocritical."

"Of course not, Mr. Vale."

He smiled widely, enjoying her teasing tone.

As they slowly made their way toward her front porch together, they loosely held hands again, which felt completely natural to both of them. As usual, being herself with Michael was totally effortless and Rebecca began dreading having to say goodbye to him again.

As they reached the front door, she reached for her keys and wondered if he felt the same way she did. She unlocked the door, replaced the keys in her purse, and turned to face him. He was standing slightly closer than she had expected as she looked up into his beautiful brown eyes, and without warning, the nervous girl from the bookstore returned.

In the blink of an eye, her heart began to race as it had the first night they'd met.

Seeming to pick up on the sudden change in emotional atmosphere, he subtly kept his distance as he spoke.

"So... I should let you get inside."

She understood his cautious tone and logically agreed with it, but a tiny part of her was slightly disappointed.

"Yes, I guess so. Thanks again for today."

"You're welcome. It was nice to see you smile so much today. I really enjoyed being with you."

For a moment he seemed to want to say something more but stopped himself. Instead he locked eyes with her, looking more serious and determined.

"Until next time?"

Despite how comfortable she'd felt with him all afternoon, he still had the ability to send her reeling with one look.

"That would be nice." She struggled to keep her voice even.

He gently placed both hands on her shoulders and slowly pulled her closer to him, softly kissing the top of her head, clearly struggling with his own self-restraint.

# Behind the Glass

"I'll call you soon," he whispered into her hair. He gently released her and stepped back a little, allowing her to open the front door and step inside.

She looked back at him before closing the door, smiling contently.

"Good night, Michael."

He returned the smile and seemed somewhat reluctant to leave her.

"Good night, Rebecca."

As he turned and walked back to his truck, she slowly closed the door then hurried to the window to watch him drive away until he was out of sight.

Sinking into her couch with a huge grin still on her face, she was completely astonished at what a difference a day could make.

# CHAPTER EIGHT

*Discovery*

The tiny specks of acrylic paint scattered in his dark brown tousled hair and all over his ripped jeans and black t-shirt were usually a sign that it had been a good morning. As Michael slowly stepped back to survey the painting he had finally finished, he felt a rare sense of accomplishment.

As a typically self-critical artist, he was rarely completely satisfied with anything he had created, but this painting was different, set apart from anything he'd ever done. His growing preoccupation with Rebecca had resulted in frequent bursts of artistic inspiration, and this work of art, along with many others he'd created since meeting her, was tangible proof of that.

For the past several weeks, after waking at sunrise each morning to help the staff at Vale Ranch feed and water the horses, he made certain to set aside a few hours to escape to his private artist's loft to paint. It had become the most essential part of his day.

On the eastern edge of the property, tucked behind one of the main stables, his loft was a simple barn-style building that the family had converted as a surprise for him during high school after he began showing such a strong interest in art. At the time, the interior was a fairly rugged, unfinished looking space, but the high ceilings, exposed wood beams, and large open windows they had custom installed made a perfect space to create his art.

While Michael was in college, after spending only one year in a dorm on campus, he and his father had built a loft space in the barn for him to live in permanently. He had quickly discovered he missed the peace and quiet of the country during his first semester at UW Madison, and hadn't cared for the wild fraternity scene that much. He also missed being able to paint whenever the mood struck him, and found himself driving home more and more.

These days, the renovated barn had become his permanent home and was now completely finished in a modest decor. Grace had gladly made it one of her personal home decorating projects after the loft was finished, and Michael enjoyed collaborating with her on it. He lived simply and didn't require much beyond the basic amenities, yet the space felt rustically stylish nonetheless. Grace had always had a flare for interior design.

As he stood in silence critiquing his latest creation, he felt the warmth of the late morning sun beaming in through the large eastern window. He glanced over at the clock realizing that it was close to ten already. He now had only two hours left to wait before he'd finally see her again.

A week earlier Rebecca had finally accepted his invitation to spend a day with him at the ranch this weekend. The opportunity to photograph Vale Ranch on a gorgeous spring day was impossible to resist, and she seemed more eager and inspired than ever to add to her portfolio now that she was being taken seriously as an artist.

She'd met with Ethan's friend, Dominic, the owner of Mystic Art, a few days earlier and was waiting to hear back from him. It was all happening so fast, and Michael was grateful she felt comfortable confiding in him on a regular basis. They talked for hours on the phone at times, almost every day since he'd brought her to Behind the Glass.

It had been two weeks since her gallery opening, yet to him it felt as if it were only yesterday. It had truly been an incredible evening together, one neither of them would ever forget, and he felt they had connected in a way they never had before. He longed to see her sooner than today but had continued keeping his distance, giving her space.

Admittedly, he wanted more with her but was content with their growing friendship and loved their long talks about art and daily life. She had a wonderful sense of humour and a similar outlook on life. With each passing day he slowly learned more about her; he became more certain that he wanted to build a life with her. Now more than ever, she had become his first thought every morning and his last every night. And today at last, he'd see her again in person.

# Behind the Glass

After he'd showered and made all of the necessary arrangements for their day together, he made his way to the stables on the highest point of the property. From there he could see the long meandering gravel driveway that led to the main road from the ranch while he prepared his two favourite horses, Duke and Piper, for their ride later.

He had offered to pick her up at her house in Madison, but she insisted on driving herself. She didn't elaborate much, but it seemed that coming back here after so many years would likely stir long forgotten childhood memories of her parents' divorce. Despite his own desire to drive her here himself, he understood completely and respected her privacy.

As he strode down the path from the stables to Sawyer Lodge, the largest building on the property that housed the dining hall and main gathering den, he caught a glimpse of a faint dust cloud in the distance on the gravel driveway.

Finally seeing her car driving toward the ranch after nearly a week of restless anticipation stirred an excitement in him he'd never known.

Rebecca was finally here, at his home, and he couldn't wait to show her everything.

He stepped out onto the large wooden porch of the lodge, watching her car gradually approach into the main parking lot. She parked at the base of the main stair, just below where Michael was standing, and gave him a familiar relaxed smile the instant their eyes met. It actually reminded him of how she had always smiled at Leo, which was encouraging.

"Hi!" she called out sweetly as she stepped out of her car and approached him. He could hear the subtle excitement in her voice. He returned the smile, casually walking down the stairs, trying to contain his own excitement.

"Hi," he said as they met at the base of the stairs on the main walkway. He gave her a relaxed, gentle hug. Her amazing scent was exhilarating, as always.

"How was the drive?"

"It was actually pretty awesome. I had forgotten how picturesque Wisconsin was out in the country in the spring. Mazomanie is such a gorgeous area."

"Well, I'm glad you enjoyed it. It turned out to be a beautiful day."

That was an understatement. In the fresh warm air and mid-day sunlight, she looked stunning. She wore faded jeans, light brown riding boots, and a loose, light green tank top. A simple silver necklace with an abstract silver charm hung delicately around her neck. Her long flowing light brown hair blew freely in the breeze, and she looked relaxed and happy as she surveyed her surroundings, taking in the scenery.

"It's been years since I've been here but it all looks the same and feels so *familiar.*"

She looked up at the custom celestial sun and moon weathervane at the top of the largest stable next to the main riding ring.

# Behind the Glass

"Oh my God, it's still there. I always loved that weathervane."

Michael was amused that she focused on this particular detail, and loved seeing her youthful side coming out as she spoke.

"Yeah, that's been there forever. My Aunt Felicia's contribution when the stables were renovated. She and Grace are responsible for any of the more feminine finishing touches around here." They both always had an innate ability of transforming a house into a home.

He led her gently by the hand as they slowly began walking the property together. Rebecca continued to take in her surroundings and almost looked lost in thought from time to time. He simply watched her quietly, wondering what she was thinking about and if her childhood memories were surfacing.

"This place is so peaceful and welcoming, just like I remember it from when I was a girl. I'll admit I'm having quite a déjà vu moment right now." She seemed somewhat lost in her own world for a little while and spoke as if trying to recall every detail. "I remember staying in that building over there," she said pointing to one of the bunkhouses, "and my horse was in that stable over there. I think her name was Buttercup... or something."

"Butterscotch. I rode her a lot when I was younger. She was a good horse and one of my favourites over the years. She had a really gentle soul and wouldn't hurt a flea. We usually assigned her to girls and younger kids, beginners, because she was incredibly calm."

"Yes, she was. I remember that about her. And pregnant too, if I recall correctly." She giggled as if remembering something amusing. "She had quite an appetite!"

"That's entirely possible," Michael laughed. "She was a mare we bred several times. We actually still own one of her brood, another mare named Scout. I'll introduce you later if you'd like. She's a lot like her mother in temperament; you'd like her."

They slowly made their way past the two main riding rings where two trainers exercised and trained several horses, past the four bunkhouses and two lower stables, onto the winding trail that led to the two higher stables overlooking the rolling fields. Michael added comments here and there as they toured the grounds, and Rebecca asked an occasional question, but they eventually fell into a comfortable rhythm, completely in synch with one another, simply enjoying the walk together. As Michael reacquainted her with the ranch she hadn't seen in years, she seemed completely relaxed.

Rebecca casually strolled over to the rustic split rail fence near the entrance to one of the stables on the higher end of the property and admired the breath-taking view of the countryside. Michael joined her and smiled the instant their eyes finally met. He simply couldn't contain how amazing he felt at this moment, finally being with her here in the home he loved.

She gave him a puzzled look as if trying to read his mind.

"So, what's the plan for today? You didn't say much on the phone, which makes me wonder what you're up to." She furrowed her brow and smiled mischievously.

"Well, you said that you'd like to add to your portfolio, so I thought I'd take you out for a ride in the country. I'll take you wherever your photographer's eye wants to go, and you can shoot to your heart's content. The horses are ready for us and I've had your camera bag brought up while we were on our walk. I hope you don't mind."

As much as he loved surprising her with things, he was still somewhat cautious, careful not to overstep any boundaries. In this case however, he seemed to hit the mark perfectly. She was positively beaming and obviously touched by his thoughtfulness.

"No not at all, that sounds wonderful. But it's been a while since I've ridden. You'll have to be patient with me..." Her sudden modesty was adorable as always.

"You'll be fine, trust me. It's like riding a bike. It'll come back to you, I promise."

He had assumed she probably wasn't an experienced rider and planned on taking some of the easier trails for their ride. He had also selected one of their best horses for her. Riding Piper was like riding a horse with power steering, and she was as gentle and intelligent as they came.

"Okay, I trust you." She looked over his shoulder at the stables with a raised brow. "Are we going now?" The excited young girl who adored horses was starting to emerge, and Michael felt an overwhelming need to give her anything she wanted in the world.

"That's the plan. Come on, I'd like to introduce you to someone."

He took her by the hand and led her into the beautiful stable. Finished tastefully in polished wood and black metal trim at each stall, it was a simple wood structure with a long wide corridor, open at each end. Ten stalls lined each side of the corridor with an open central space for hay storage. Smells of leather, hay, and horses filled the space, yet the stable appeared extremely clean and pristine. Sounds of soft neighs, snorts, and nickers from the many horses housed there created a constant melody.

He led her to the fourth stall on the left and opened the sliding stall door. A gorgeous chestnut Arabian mare with a light caramel mane and a delicate white stripe down her nose stood before them as he led her further inside the stall. She was a younger horse with a sleek, lean build and extremely kind eyes.

"This is Piper. You'll be riding her today."

Wide eyed, Rebecca slowly approached her and gently placed her hand on her neck.

"Hey girl," she began as she looked into her beautiful chocolate brown eyes. "Aren't you just the most *beautiful* thing?"

Piper nickered quietly and took a small step toward Rebecca, leaning in toward her slightly. Rebecca looked over to Michael and smiled, shrugging her shoulders.

"That's her way of saying hello to you. I think she likes you."

Michael was pleased he chose correctly. Grace may have inherited the ability to match people together but no one could match horses to people better than Michael. He knew the personalities and idiosyncrasies of every horse they owned and boarded at Vale Ranch, and could always be depended upon to match campers with horses at every orientation. It was definitely a gift.

"She's amazing, Michael. I can't wait to ride her." She began stroking her neck softly while looking into her gentle eyes. "She seems so calm, so sweet."

"She is. She's an incredibly gentle horse and loves taking care of her riders. She has a broad back and a remarkably smooth trot. She's so comfortable to ride that some of the riders actually call her the 'comfy couch.' I thought she'd be the perfect horse for you today."

Piper leaned into Rebecca again and nickered quietly as she lowered her head slightly.

"What's she doing now?"

"She's trying to tell you she likes what you're doing and wants her ears scratched. It's her favourite thing in the world. She's warming up to you quicker than I thought she would. She must really like you."

Obviously Michael wasn't the only one immediately drawn to her.

"How funny, I never realized horses could be so expressive."

She began scratching Piper's ears while the horse stood completely motionless, almost in a trace, clearly enjoying it.

"Wow, she does like this!" Rebecca seemed to enjoy it as much as Piper.

"Well, I'll leave you two for a minute while I go get Duke."

"I assume Duke is the horse you'll be riding?" she asked with a raised brow.

"Yes, Duke is actually my horse. He hasn't been ridden much by the campers because he's better with more experienced riders. We've only had him for about a year now, and I'm still training him. He's got an independent personality and likes to move at his own pace. I'm one of the only riders he really responds to, so for now he's all mine."

"He sounds like someone else I know," Rebecca teased.

Michael smiled, shaking his head as he walked across the main corridor to Duke's stall. He could feel Rebecca's eyes on him as he opened the sliding stall door and enjoyed knowing she was looking at him.

Duke gave Michael a loud blow with his nose the moment he saw him opening the door.

"I know, boy, settle down. We'll be on the trails soon enough," he murmured as he reached for his mouth. He fed him a treat and stroked his neck as he looked into his dark eyes.

Duke was a stunning black pinto stallion with a perfectly marked black and white coat. Other than his white lower legs, known as stockings, white mane, and a small white stripe on his nose, he was entirely jet black with beautiful dark eyes. Much larger than Piper, he had a stout build with a thick muscular neck and hind quarters.

As Michael led him out of the stall, Duke gave another nose blow and nickered quietly, clearly anticipating the upcoming ride. Michael glanced at Rebecca, shooting her a quick grin.

Still giving Piper a nice scratch, Rebecca had been admiring Duke from across the aisle.

"Michael, he's absolutely beautiful!" She seemed completely mesmerized.

"Yeah, he's pretty amazing, isn't he? My father bought him from a good friend of ours in Colorado last year, and we couldn't be happier with him. He's definitely become one of my all-time favourites. Just wait until you see him on the trails."

Michael tied Duke to a nearby post and began saddling him while Rebecca watched his every movement. After the saddle was in place, he placed her camera bag in a small saddle bag he had fastened onto Duke.

"I'll take good care of this for you, okay?"

He assumed Rebecca trusted him with her camera, but because it had become her most valued possession these days, he wanted to reassure her anyway.

"That's fine, I trust you," she answered as she carefully led Piper to him.

He considered teaching her how to saddle Piper herself, but decided against it for today. She was clearly a little self-conscious about her riding ability, and he didn't want to make any aspect of today remotely uncomfortable for her. He also, as usual in her presence, had an overwhelming need to care for her in any way he could.

After both horses were saddled and ready for the ride, Michael gently helped Rebecca onto Piper just outside the entrance to the stable. As she familiarized herself with being on a horse again after so many years, he could see the exhilaration in her eyes. She seemed unexpectedly confident and totally at ease. With a light breeze blowing through her hair, she looked down at him with the most gorgeous smile he'd ever seen.

"Well, look at you." Michael quickly mounted Duke with a swiftness that came from a lifetime of riding horses. It was as natural as breathing to him. "So, are you ready to ride?"

# Behind the Glass

"Definitely, lead the way," she beamed as she gave Piper a quick pat. "I think Piper will take good care of me today."

"I'm sure she will. Just follow me and let me know if you'd like to stop along the way. We'll be walking most of the trails so you can really enjoy the scenery, but we'll speed up to a trot when you're ready, okay?"

He wanted to establish her comfort zone with Piper, and get her used to riding again, as he would with any beginner, but part of him was simply being overly cautious. Admittedly, he couldn't seem to help himself where she was concerned.

"That sounds great, thanks." She sounded somewhat relieved.

Michael led Duke along the winding split rail fence, down a gentle hill to a narrow opening that led to a large open field. Once in the field, they walked along an immense tree line to a marked opening at the edge of the forest leading to an uphill trail. A portion of the trail was steep, but Michael carefully led them through a series of switchbacks, glancing back at Rebecca occasionally to make sure she was comfortable with Piper.

As the trail began to level out, they rode quietly for several minutes until they came to a large opening in the trees that overlooked a peaceful meandering stream with an aged wooden footbridge covered in moss. Michael led Duke off the trail to a flat grassy clearing as Piper leisurely followed. The forest was completely silent other than the quiet bubbling of the stream below and the occasional chirps of chickadees and warblers above.

"I thought we'd stop here for a bit."

Looking up into the trees, Rebecca appeared to be in another world.

"It's so beautiful. This place is so peaceful. I can see why you love it here so much."

After they each dismounted Duke and Piper, Michael led the horses to a nearby post to tie them up. He gave them each a gentle pat and retrieved Rebecca's camera bag, as she wandered toward the footbridge. He joined her and handed her the bag.

"This is one of my favourite places. The subject matter is endless. I'm sure you'll have no problem adding to your portfolio out here."

She marvelled at the ethereal space around them and smiled as their eyes met.

"Thanks," she said taking her bag. "Yes, it's hard to know where to start actually."

He sensed she was looking at everything through her artist's eye and was getting deeper in thought trying to decide what to capture on film. He could appreciate this feeling completely, recalling distant memories of painting still lifes out here early in his career.

"Well, I'll leave you to it. Take your time, we have all day."

Rebecca looked confused.

"Where are *you* going?"

# Behind the Glass

Her uncertain furrowed brow was an expression that always made him smile instantly.

"Don't worry, I'm not going anywhere. I brought a blanket along in case we wanted to stop for a while. I'm just going to hang out over there so I'm not in your way."

"Oh, okay. Thanks." She seemed relieved.

As Michael made his way back toward the horses, he could feel her eyes on him again. He untied the hand woven wool blanket from Duke's saddle, laid it out on the ground and took a seat while Rebecca slowly began photographing at the edge of the stream.

He had intended to read a book so she wouldn't feel uncomfortable, but watching her work was fascinating. At first she seemed somewhat self-conscious having him nearby, looking back at him every so often, but after a while, the photographer slowly took over.

She expertly adjusted the settings on the camera, changed the focus, checked the lighting, and altered the angle several times before shooting, as if the camera was an extension of her. She moved swiftly, surveying each scene from multiple angles, moving down stream and then upstream, sometimes changing the subject matter entirely, searching for the perfect shot. She climbed part way up a tree at one point, and then slouched down so low near the water that Michael worried she'd fall in.

She seemed almost detached from everything in the world except her art, and appeared utterly carefree. He had witnessed this unburdened side of her before and was wantonly getting caught up in it again. Completely mesmerized by this amazing woman he now couldn't imagine living life without, he hadn't even opened the book he was still holding in his hands.

It was honestly one of the most intriguing experiences he'd ever had, watching an artist work but from the opposite end of the spectrum. Grace had always loved watching him paint when they were growing up, but until now he never completely understood the allure.

Once she felt satisfied she'd captured the images she was after, Rebecca broke away and walked toward him, noticing the wondrous look in his eyes as she approached him. Feeling slightly self-conscious, she stopped and smiled.

"Have you been watching me the *whole* time?"

"I couldn't help it. Seeing you work is... impressive."

He expected her typically embarrassed response but instead she smiled proudly.

"Well, in that case I have a favour to ask of you."

"You do?" he hesitated, trying to read her eyes. "Okay, what can I do for you?"

She smiled widely and playfully held the camera to her eye. "Smile!"

"Seriously?"

"Seriously," she asserted. "This is something I've wanted to do for a while."

# Behind the Glass

Captivated by her energy he complied without hesitation.

Without a word she effortlessly slipped back into her radiantly creative persona and began thoughtfully clicking images of him while he continued admiring her in awe. Slowly with each shot, the energy between them transformed from casual and playful to more serious and reflective. His smile faded and his expression became more pensive and intense.

Picking up on this, Rebecca slowly lowered her camera, walked over to him, and sat down on the blanket beside him. She held his gaze for a long moment and breathed deeply as if calming herself before she spoke, "Do you remember when I left you at the wedding reception after our dance?"

It was a moment he had thought about often, a moment he would never forget.

"Yes."

"I told you to stay there because I had to go get something."

"I remember."

"With everything that happened after... I never told you my plan."

"Your plan?"

"Yes. I had promised Leo and Isabel I'd take some black and whites for their wedding day. I left you that night to go to the coatroom to get my camera bag." She paused for a moment recalling the memory. "I had planned on taking some pictures of you too."

He hesitated before he spoke, seeing a glimmer of anguish in her eyes.

"But you never got the chance."

"No, I didn't."

She looked off in the distance for a few moments, reflecting on the events of that evening. As upsetting as her unfortunate discovery that evening had been, Michael couldn't help being wholly thankful for what had unfolded later that night and in the weeks that followed.

Had she not gone back to the coatroom for her camera, they wouldn't be sitting here together now. Sometimes in life, things really did happen for a reason.

She looked back to him and smiled softly, appearing more relaxed. The peace and solitude of the surrounding forest seemed to comfort her.

"Thank you for that, for letting me photograph you. While I enjoy shooting landscapes, there is nothing more inspiring than getting human expression on film. There's something about the process that's so... fluid, so exciting. It's actually what got me started as a photographer."

Thinking back to Rebecca's portfolio on the walls of Behind the Glass, her portraits definitely stood out in comparison to the rest of her work. It was clearly her passion.

"I've seen your work and I understand what you mean. You definitely have a gift for it. Your portraits are compelling."

# Behind the Glass

Michael could identify with her preference in subject matter, and had always favoured portrait over landscape art, especially in recent months. He truly believed something exceptional could be created from studying the human form.

"Thank you. It's definitely something I'd like to keep exploring. Honestly, I still feel like I have so much to learn." His compliments always seemed to bring out her modesty.

She had unintentionally given him an opportunity to inquire about something he had never known exactly how to ask.

"You seem to know what you're doing, at least from my perspective. Are you self-taught or did you go to photography school?"

Amazingly it had never come up during their many conversations about art and it was something he had wondered.

"A little of both, actually."

She placed her timeworn camera in between them on the blanket and smiled as she ran her hand over it gently.

"I had always enjoyed taking pictures with my family growing up, but my love of photography really started during my junior year of high school when I took an introductory photography class. I actually learned enough during that year to convert our entire laundry room into a dark room for developing my own prints.

"It was amazing. I had never enjoyed creating anything so much in my life, and would literally spend hours, even days, developing film and learning the process. My mom helped me look into art schools and after high school I went to the Milwaukee Institute of Art and Design for my BFA in Photography for two years."

She paused for a moment, pondering the next inevitable question.

"Two years? I take it you didn't finish?" Michael didn't miss a beat.

"No, not yet. My mom ran into financial trouble, and my younger brother Trey had been accepted on a partial scholarship to UW Madison's medical program. He's an extremely gifted kid, with straight A's and had graduated high school a year early. His dream has always been to go into medicine, and my mom could only afford so much."

"So you dropped out of school for him?" Her self-sacrifice was humbling.

"It was supposed to be temporary until I could secure my own financial aid, but it hasn't exactly worked out that way. I still plan on finishing when the time is right."

He wondered why she hadn't mentioned her father's role in all of this, but assumed she had her reasons. She hadn't talked about him much other than the fact that he lived far away and she didn't have much contact with him. Regardless, her determination to make it on her own was admirable.

# Behind the Glass

He found himself thoroughly fascinated and wanting to know more.

"So for now you're getting all the practical experience you can?"

"Something like that." She shot him a teasing smile. "Learning by doing ..."

He returned the smile, recalling their previous conversation.

"Well, I'd say it's working out for you nicely so far."

"Yes, I've been incredibly lucky," she admitted.

They both slowly stood up, ready to get back on the trails again. Michael shook out the blanket, rolled it up and tied it to Duke's saddle.

As he gently helped Rebecca onto Piper again, he stopped and gently held her hand for a long moment, looking up into her gorgeous green eyes. The flawless natural radiance of her delicate face reflected her innocence in that moment.

"Luck had *nothing* to do with it Rebecca, trust me."

She stared back at him speechless, visibly moved by emotion. He slowly released her hand and took her camera bag from her. He untied the horses and placed her camera in the saddle bag before mounting Duke. He peered back at her, admiring her magnificent beauty in the shadows and broken sunlight of the forest.

"Are you ready to keep going? I have more to show you."

"Yes." She seemed somewhat lost in thought for a moment but eventually focused back to him. "This place was wonderful. I can't wait to see what's next."

He looked deeply into her eyes for a long moment before steering Duke onto the path, smiling contently at the fact that she seemed as affected by him now as she had been the first night they met.

He slowly led Duke out of the grassy clearing toward the stream and over the simple wooden bridge. They followed the water's edge for a short time until a subtle trail revealed itself. Slowly, they rode deeper into the lush foliage and uneven terrain until they eventually came to a long flat trail.

He slowed a bit and turned back to Rebecca, who seemed extremely at ease, enjoying the scenic expanse surrounding them.

"Are you ready to speed up to a trot?"

Her face instantly lit up.

"Definitely!"

"Okay, sit up straight with your heels down and keep your hands close and steady, shortening the reins a little. Piper will follow Duke's lead so when you're ready to go, give her a gentle squeeze with your legs. Relax your back, hips, and legs once we get going, and the ride will feel smoother."

Still unsure of how much she remembered from her childhood riding lessons, he didn't want to take any chances with her safety.

Rebecca adjusted herself as he'd instructed and seemed eager to go.

# Behind the Glass

"It's been a while, but it's all slowly coming back to me." She raised her brow and smiled. "Thank you, Mr. Vale."

He laughed, shaking his head.

"Alright, here we go."

With one experienced fluid motion, Michael shifted Duke's walk to a trot while Piper and Rebecca easily followed suit. The pair rode quietly on the grassy trail, keeping a relaxed steady rhythm as the trees raced by and the exhilarating wind flowed through them in gentle waves. They were each in perfect sync with their horses as a familiar invisible bond of unconditional trust formed between horse and rider.

As the trail inclined slightly, their pace quickened. Michael glanced back, checking on Rebecca from time to time, and found her keeping up perfectly, completely confident. She had obviously found her comfort level with Piper and was thoroughly enjoying herself. Much like watching her dance or create art she was definitely in her element, utterly relaxed and radiantly happy.

As they approached a steeper, narrower portion of the trail, the sound of rushing water could faintly be heard in the distance. Michael gradually slowed to a walk as the trail began winding with the contours of the large lush hillside before them. They steadily made their way upward to the crest of the hill that gradually levelled out onto a long flat ridge covered in a sea of wild flowers overlooking a small body of water.

As the sound of flowing water below grew louder, Michael led them to a small grassy clearing immediately off the trail to a weathered hand carved hitching post. He swiftly dismounted Duke and quietly tied the horses up while Rebecca dismounted Piper, looking around curiously.

"This place is amazing. I can hear the water but can't tell where it's coming from."

Michael grabbed the blanket and the camera bag, smiling as their eyes met.

"It's not far. We'll go the rest of the way on foot."

Michael attached a leather carrying strap to each end of the rolled blanket and slung it over his head and shoulder along with the camera bag. The terrain on some of the trails ahead was somewhat unstable and he preferred her to be completely unencumbered. He gave each of the horses a light scratch while watching Rebecca slowly wander among the delicately coloured wild flowers, taking in the view of the small lake below.

"I don't think I ever came up here when I stayed at the ranch. I definitely would remember this place."

"No, you probably wouldn't have. We keep this part of the property semi-private. A few of our campers have been out here, but it's usually off limits to anyone but family and friends. You'll see why when we get down there."

# Behind the Glass

He gently took her hand and led her along the verdurous ridge to a steep trail made of crude stone steps leading toward the water. As the steps gradually faded into a rugged dirt and root-ridden path, he tightened his grip on her hand, carefully leading her toward the level grassy trail below.

The sound of the roaring water grew much louder as they slowly continued on the winding footpath through the thick foliage. As they finally reached the tranquil shoreline of the lake, they paused near another steep set of stone steps along the bank.

"Careful here, it gets pretty steep. Watch your footing and hold onto me if you need to."

Rebecca followed him cautiously, firmly holding onto his hand and muscular forearm with both her hands, trusting him completely. He took his time, steadily holding her hand, making sure she was balanced and had a solid footing as they gradually descended the rocky passageway. As they finally reached the bottom, a modest yet roaring waterfall came into view beside them.

Spreading out over a wide ledge surrounded by formations of weathered mossy bedrock, the small lake above spilled over the edge like a smooth wall of glass, plunging several feet below and thundering into the placid waters of a large pool that fed into an adjacent winding creek. The waterfall was flanked by a thick forest on the farther bank, and a flat open clearing resembling a small amphitheatre on the opposite bank was surrounded by tall cliffs of bedrock. A large arrangement of man-made log benches surrounded a massive beautifully crafted stone fire pit facing the water's edge.

Rebecca stood still for a few moments, surveying the beauty before her.

"This is incredible. What *is* this place?"

"For lack of a better word, our backyard."

She smiled, cocking her head slightly.

"Your backyard?"

"It's the best description we've come up with."

He slowly led her toward the gathering area as she gave him a curious smile.

"Our life here at Vale Ranch isn't exactly private. The kids who stay with us for weeks at a time become part of our family when they're here. The ranch has always been based on that philosophy, and we make sure the kids feel completely at home with us."

"I remember. I certainly did."

They sat down beside one another on one of the benches.

"And they should. For most of them it's their first experience away from home. Above all else, we *always* put the kids first. But imagine having house guests almost year round."

She raised her brow, giving him a sympathetic look. "I can only imagine."

"We all love what we do for the kids here at the ranch, and wouldn't have it any other way, but living where we work can sometimes be consuming. We need a little something, a special place, just for us once in a while. And this is it."

She smiled and giggled quietly as she looked around, shaking her head.

"What's so funny?"

"So you have a *hideout* of your own huh?" she teased sweetly.

The irony of it made him smile, thinking of the countless times he'd come here to escape. It was astonishing to him that he hadn't made that connection until now. Fundamentally they were more similar than he realized at times.

He nodded his head thoughtfully in admittance.

"Apparently so. I'd never really seen it that way, but you're absolutely right. I usually come here to clear my head. It's always been one of my favourite places."

"An oasis," she stated simply. She obviously could relate completely.

"Exactly. Is that what Behind the Glass is for you?"

"It was," she paused, looking up into his eyes, "but not anymore."

"No? Why not?"

She looked down briefly, collecting her thoughts before she spoke.

"I did go there to escape, to hide. You seemed to know that even before I was willing to admit it to myself. Behind the Glass will always be an incredibly special place to me. But I don't feel like I have to go there to hide anymore."

"Is that because you were hiding from Brett?"

"Partially. But it wasn't just Brett I was hiding from. It was a lot of things. Mainly I think I was hiding from myself in a way. Escaping was my way of trying to control something that can't be controlled. It's taken me a while to realize that."

She looked as if she wanted to say more but stopped herself. Saying these things out loud was obviously a big step for her and something he didn't expect.

"What were you trying to control?"

As she looked at him she suddenly seemed shy and cautious.

"A fear that's been with me most of my life I think..." She slowly looked down again.

She lightly ran her finger over the silver charm on her necklace and gently held it in between two fingers. As she released it back onto her neck again, it caught Michael's eye. At first glance it appeared to be merely an abstract silver charm, but after further examination he could see that it was actually a delicate pendant depicting a mother holding hands with two children in a heart shaped embrace. It obviously meant a great deal to her.

"What are you afraid of Rebecca?"

She took a deep breath and stared at the waterfall for a long while before she spoke.

"Being hurt. Being left behind again. Opening myself up to someone."

"Did Brett know you felt this way? I assume he didn't know about your Friday nights."

She looked back at him with guilty eyes.

"No, I have to admit that I wasn't very open with him about my true feelings. That's never been easy for me. I've just never been very good at it."

"Have you ever talked to *anyone* about your true feelings?"

"Other than my mom, no."

"Even Leo?"

"No, not really. Maybe years ago when we were kids, but not now."

"But, you're talking to *me* ..."

"I know." She looked away, focusing on the waterfall again. "And it scares me."

Turning to face her, he gently took both her hands in his, looking at her with determined eyes. She turned slightly toward him, only looking down at their hands.

"It shouldn't. You don't have to be scared, ever, with me." He spoke slowly with a calm reassuring voice. "You can tell me as much or as little as you want, okay?"

He waited patiently as she finally looked up into his eyes with a gentle trusting smile.

"Okay."

Slowly she described bits and pieces of her childhood and her parents' divorce. She focused on how important her mom and brother, Trey, were to her and how her mom had been an amazing source of support throughout her life. She touched briefly on her almost non-existent relationship with her father, and how he lived in Chicago with her step-mom and half-sister, Amanda, the product of his infidelity.

She described her life-long relationship with Leo, and how he had always looked out for her, and summarized the few short relationships she'd had before Brett. She told him how Leo had always wanted to see her happy and how he had introduced her to Brett several months ago. She didn't go into much detail but it seemed they had a fairly happy and normal relationship until she caught him cheating in a coatroom at her best friend's wedding. She omitted the details but he could sense the humiliation she had felt wasn't far from the surface, even now. He also quickly understood the parallels between Brett's unfaithfulness and her father's.

Gradually, the more she told him, the calmer she appeared, as if a huge weight was finally being lifted. As he learned more about her past and slowly understood her feelings and fears, an almost uncontrollable need to hold her in his arms and never let her go washed over him. Resisting this sudden urge, he continued to steadily hold her delicate hands in his while listening intently to every word, feeling extremely grateful for her decision to open up to him little by little.

She paused, smiling warmly, breathing a huge sigh of relief.

"You've been so quiet, just letting me go on and on. Thank you."

"I'm just happy you feel comfortable talking to me like this."

"I do. I always have," she reflected briefly and smiled, "since the first night we met."

He smiled, thinking back to that night, remembering their first conversation and how they had connected so quickly. "Well, despite your reasons for being there each week, I don't think I'll ever be able to express how thankful I am that you chose Grace's shop as your oasis."

She subtly tightened her grip on his hands. "Me too."

As she beamed up at him with the most contented smile he'd seen today, he felt another sudden almost irrepressible urge to take her in his arms. He was quite sure however that it wasn't the right moment, not yet at least. She had taken a huge step telling him as much as she had and it was crucial that they take things slowly. Despite how amazing he imagined it would be to have her in his arms and even feel her lips on his, he was a patient man and needed to know for certain that she was ready for that.

Likely sensing what he was thinking, based on her tentative expression, she subtly glanced over to the gushing waterfall. It looked absolutely stunning in the late afternoon sunlight and he knew she'd want to capture it while it lasted.

Something seemed to suddenly catch her eye. "Oh wow, look at that!"

She had an adorable almost childlike expression on her face.

At the right angle a beautiful delicate rainbow could be seen in the mist immediately next to the falling water. The amber sunbeams made the entire scene appear otherworldly.

"You might want to catch that now before the sunlight shifts its angle. It'll only last for a few minutes." He slowly released her hands, secretly wishing he could hold them forever.

Hesitating briefly, she gently stood up as he handed her the camera bag. She made her way to the water's edge, quietly deciding how best to shoot the scene. After several minutes of carefully photographing the waterfall from every conceivable angle, she had gradually slipped back into her artistic persona again while he enjoyed watching her every move from afar.

She took full advantage of her surroundings, stopping only briefly to change the film in her camera a few times, then continuing to shoot as much as possible before the sun began its eventual decent in the cloudless sky.

Before she finished for the day, she slyly took a few of Michael too, giving him a teasing silly smile as she did so. He laughed, smiling easily.

# Behind the Glass

"That's perfect! Keep doing that. I love your smile."

"You do, huh?" He couldn't help but smile. Watching her, being here with her, being *anywhere* with her, brought it out naturally. He was continually astounded at how unbelievably happy she made him feel.

After several clicks of her camera she lowered it and paused, looking more serious.

"Today was amazing, Michael. You have no idea how much I've enjoyed being here."

Her expression gradually changed again looking unexpectedly unguarded, reminding him of the delicate, demure girl from the bookstore. Something in her eyes inherently called to him as it had the first time he'd seen her.

Without a word he stood up and slowly walked over to her, holding her unwavering gaze until they were standing only inches apart. Her eyes widened as she peered up at him. He hesitated for a moment, trying to read her eyes before gently wrapping his arms around her. As he drew her closer, she slowly rested her head on his chest. He softly stroked her hair and delicately kissed the top of her head. As she nuzzled into him, she wrapped her arms around his waist, hugging him tightly and breathing a long contented sigh.

"I'm glad you came today too," he whispered into her hair.

Having her in his arms, feeling her return his tight embrace so intently, made him realize how complete he felt with her in his life, as if she had been the missing part of himself he'd been searching for all along. It was a surprisingly overwhelming feeling, but one he'd gladly get used to and never grow tired of.

As the soothing sounds of the waterfall echoed into the calm beauty of the forest, they continued to hold each other for a long while, neither of them moving or wanting to let go.

The sun was fading and he knew their time here would have to end soon. They needed to get back to the stables before dark and based on the time of day, should start making their way back very shortly. He hated more than anything than to release her but didn't want to have her riding in darkness either.

"We should probably head back soon," he whispered.

"I had a feeling you'd say that," she whispered back.

She obviously didn't want the moment to end either, which made him smile.

Slowly they broke away from each other, joined only by their hands, gazing at one another with the same gentle contented smile.

Rebecca gave the waterfall one last long gaze as Michael slung the blanket and camera bag over his head and shoulder again. When he sensed she was ready to leave, he took her by the hand and led her carefully back up the steep trails to the horses on the floral ridge.

They rode back along the long trails together in silence, alternating walking and trotting with the gorgeous glowing sunset at their backs. He glanced back to her from time to time, noticing a certain calm about her in comparison to their previous ride. She seemed quiet and reflective, almost lost in her own thoughts.

They reached the stables at dusk and by the time Michael settled the horses back into their stalls, the temperature had dropped slightly. Rebecca helped him feed and water Duke and Piper, along with all of the other horses in the stables as nightfall slowly settled around them.

After Michael finished up and closed the last stable door, he glanced toward Rebecca who was standing in the center of the massive arched entrance at the far end of the stable. With her back to him while tightly hugging her arms around herself, she gazed up at the stars that were finally revealing themselves in the night sky. Her silhouette appeared so fragile, so tiny and petite from a distance. Admiring her delicate figure from afar, he also noticed her long bronze hair blowing softly in the night breeze.

Realizing that she seemed slightly chilly in her light clothing, he grabbed a nearby blanket to wrap around her shoulders before approaching her. Lost in thought, she didn't seem to hear him behind her and shivered slightly at his touch as he hugged the blanket around her. As she slowly relaxed and leaned back into his broad frame he continued to hold her closely, feeling like the luckiest man in the world.

He gently kissed the top of her head, lightly inhaling her heavenly scent.

"Thank you," he whispered.

"For what?" she whispered back.

"For today, for telling me everything you did. For trusting me."

She took a long moment, breathing deeply.

"I'm still scared, you have no idea how much, but I'm glad I told you. Honestly, I feel like I'm up on another ledge, about to jump. I want to fly more than anything, but I'm *so* afraid to fall." Her voice cracked into a faint whisper. He held her a little tighter before he spoke.

"I know you are and I can understand where it comes from, but you have to know... that I will *never* hurt you. I know those are just words right now and that you've had a lifetime of people letting you down, but I hope to be the one to change that. I've waited *so* long to find you Rebecca. Now that I finally have, I'll do whatever you need me to do to prove that to you."

She slowly turned around to face him with a look of pure disbelief in her eyes, but said nothing. Unsure of what she was thinking, he searched her expression trying to read her.

# Behind the Glass

"You just seem... too good to be true. You always have, from the first moment I saw you. It sounds crazy, but that's what makes this so scary for me. To trust something that seems so *perfect*."

She looked down, shaking her head slowly.

"I'm sorry, that probably sounds so ridiculous."

He actually understood that feeling completely.

As he thought about what she said, he finally realized why she always seemed so puzzled by his interest in her, why she never noticed how men reacted to her when she walked by, why she kept herself so guarded from anyone she'd ever dated and why she'd been so hesitant to display her artwork. She needed someone in her life to give her confidence in *herself.*

He wished there was a way he could make her understand how remarkable she was, how every little thing she did or said left him in awe of her. If she only knew how completely and irrevocably in love with her he was, maybe she'd take a chance and let go of her fears.

Before he could change his mind, he lightly placed a finger under her chin, gently willing her to look up at him again. As her beautiful wide eyes finally met his, he took her face in his hands and drew her closer, hesitating for only a second before kissing her.

As their lips gently met, the subtle electricity that had always existed between them seemed to explode all at once. His touch was tender and soft, yet there was an urgency just under the surface that neither of them could seem to control as their bodies slowly came together.

With her heart suddenly racing, she inhaled sharply and gently slid her arms around his neck, giving in to the constant longing they'd both felt for each other for months. As the blanket around her shoulders fell to their feet she gave herself over to him, letting him kiss her deeply as intense waves of emotion washed over both of them.

As their bodies pressed together, his hands slowly moved up and down her back, buried in her long hair. Trembling at his touch, her hands moved to the back of his neck as she lightly ran her fingers through his hair. Pulling her in even closer to him, he enveloped himself in her intoxicating scent, savouring the sweet taste of her mouth on his. Everywhere he touched her, her body responded to him with a flood of electricity under her skin, as liquid heat filled her veins.

Overcome with a yearning for her that came from deep within him, he kissed her with everything he had, everything he'd felt for her since the moment she'd walked into his life, everything he would ever want to be. With every pounding heartbeat, she could slowly feel herself surrendering to him as her fears began to gradually fall away, little by little.

The emotion they shared was powerful and unlike anything either of them had experienced before. Freely giving in to their feelings for one another, they both revelled in what was undoubtedly the most pure, honest moment they had ever shared together – the unmistakable sensation of truly loving someone and being loved in return, breaking down all boundaries.

Feeling startlingly fragile and exposed, Rebecca could feel the irrepressible tears she feared would come building deep inside of her and quickly filling her eyes, betraying her. Unable to control the sudden flood of emotions overpowering her, she pushed away from Michael, looking down to the ground, breathless.

"No..." she breathed. She took a step back as she spoke. "I'm sorry, I... I can't."

Michael was caught completely off guard.

"Rebecca, what's wrong?" he let out. "I'm sorry, we can slow down. Wait..."

As he reached out for her she took another step back, shaking her head, looking back at him with utter trepidation in her eyes while tears streamed down her face.

"No, I'm sorry. I thought I was ready for this. I have to go."

As panic set in, he hoped his worst fear hadn't begun to unfold before him.

"No... Rebecca, don't go. Stay here with me; it's okay."

There was desperation in his voice that surprised even him. He cautiously took another step in her direction, frantically trying to think of a way to convince her to stay.

"I'm so sorry, Michael, but I have to go," her voice trembled as tears continued to flow from her beautiful, sad eyes. "I'm not ready for this... I'm just..."

"Scared? I know you are. You don't have to be. Please don't do this."

She hugged her arms around herself looking completely unsettled and lost.

A sinking feeling in the pit of his stomach told him he had pushed too far tonight. It was too much, too soon, and deep down he knew it. Even *he* had been completely overwhelmed by what he was feeling after they'd kissed. She had opened up to him so much in such a short time today and he regretted taking it to that next level so soon. She was incredibly vulnerable tonight and on some level he knew he shouldn't have kissed her the way he did.

"I can't." she whispered, turning to walk away. "I just... I have to go."

She seemed suddenly guarded, as if trying to distance herself from what she was feeling. He tried to think of something to say to convince her to stay, but could see in her eyes that anything he said now would fall on deaf ears. She obviously needed space, and despite how much he wanted to hold her in his arms again and never let her go, he had to respect her wishes.

# Behind the Glass

"You need to know something before you go." He paused, waiting until their eyes finally met again. "I'm *here*, okay. I'm not going anywhere." He spoke slowly and calmly, hoping she'd change her mind.

She looked back at him with conflicted apologetic eyes.

"Okay."

For a fleeting moment she looked as if she'd come back to him, but instead she slowly turned around and began walking down the long stable corridor toward the opposite entrance.

With each step she took he could feel his heart aching for her.

She picked up her camera bag, paused for a moment, and looked back at him. The look in her eyes reminded him of the sad expression he'd seen so many times before as they'd parted. She was utterly torn and heartbroken.

With the words finally rising to the surface, he took a step toward her, but before he could say them she quickly turned away and disappeared out of the stable and out of sight.

For a moment he considered running after her, begging her to stay, telling her how much he loved her, but he couldn't seem to find the ability to move. He knew he had to let her go.

He also knew with as much certainty as he had ever felt in his life, that in time, she'd come back to him.

# CHAPTER NINE

## *Questions*

The road ahead was becoming nearly impossible to see in the darkness through her tears. With each passing mile that separated them, Rebecca was overcome by the piercing emptiness that was slowly consuming her. She could feel each shattered piece of herself slowly breaking apart in every direction. She held onto the steering wheel with everything she had, trying to control the unbearable waves of anguish, until finally she broke down completely and pulled over onto the side of the road, nearly crashing into a row of mailboxes.

Filled with intense regret for leaving him the way she did, she sat alone in the dim moonlight with her head buried in her hands until the uncontrollable sobbing finally subsided, desperately trying to understand what had made her run.

*How could I leave him like that?* she scolded herself. This amazing, kind, handsome man who wanted nothing more than to care for her, surely didn't deserve that from her. He had done nothing but support her since the day they'd met, in every way imaginable. And there was no mistaking his feelings for her. It was *love.*

As images of the day flooded her mind, her emotions soared, gradually absorbing what an amazing day it had been; possibly one of the best of her life. Spending such a gorgeous day at his ranch with him, simply being with him again, was something she had been looking forward to all week. Coming back there after so many years had brought back an unexpected flood of happy childhood memories, and for the first time in years she finally felt completely unburdened and at ease – with him.

She had opened up to him in a way she'd never expected, told him things about her life and herself that she hadn't told anyone before. And it felt right, all of it. Michael was, as he'd always been, remarkably easy to talk to and deep down she wanted him to know everything about her.

Even her fears... *especially* her fears.

It all felt so natural and being in his arms felt like coming home. She finally felt complete in a way she never had before in her life.

After months of waiting and longing for one another, the kiss was beyond compare.

It the most intense moment they had ever shared together, and unlike anything she had experienced before with anyone. The way he kissed her, the depth of it, left her reeling with a multitude of unexpected emotions she wasn't yet ready to face.

Feeling utterly vulnerable, she had been on the verge of giving herself to him completely, trusting him unconditionally with everything she was or ever would be. With this one kiss, he was able to gently strip away every single wall she'd spent a lifetime building to protect herself. It was easily the most overwhelming moment of her life, and left her shaken to the core.

With her guard completely down and her emotions wildly out of her control, panic had suddenly set in. Being in such emotionally unfamiliar and frightening territory for the first time in her life, her usual instinct to cut and run inevitably took over. Impulsively reacting to her deepest fears, without processing any of it, her walls came back in an instant. They were pushing away the most amazing man she'd ever had the privilege of meeting.

And she hated herself for it.

After an incredibly restless night, Rebecca slept late the next morning and spent most of the day on her couch under a blanket. Feeling completely drained and emotionally benumbed, she didn't have the slightest bit of motivation to move. She didn't eat and she barely drank. She would occasionally flip channels on the TV in an attempt to distract herself from her racing mind, but ultimately sat staring out her window at another gorgeous spring day. She sat in silence all afternoon.

Deep in thought, recalling every single remarkable detail from the previous day, she desperately tried to determine what she needed to do to overcome the fears that paralyzed her.

She longed for Michael in a way that tortured her physically. She repeatedly clutched her chest all morning each time she pictured his kind face. She was drowning and he was the oxygen she needed to survive.

She dialled Michael's number a dozen times throughout the day, but couldn't seem to find the courage to place the call. She honestly didn't know what she would say to him if he answered the phone. She couldn't imagine what he must be thinking right now.

Michael had been so wonderful, so incredibly patient with her for so long, and had given her more than she'd ever imagined since the day they'd met. Her stomach twisted and turned thinking about how she'd responded to him. She had pushed him away, rejecting him at the most pivotal moment in their relationship.

Hugging her arms tightly around herself, she shuddered at the thought of how much *she* had hurt *him*. Flashing back to the heavyhearted look on his face as she left him, she squeezed her eyes shut trying to block the most intense feelings of regret she'd ever experienced.

Rocking gently back and forth, Rebecca fought back the red hot tears brimming in her eyes. She struggled to will her mind away from that particular image of him and eventually calmed herself enough to breathe normally to sort through her thoughts and emotions.

Despite how broken she felt, down to her core, she was determined to make a plan. She had to figure out a way to get through this. Her fate was in her control. It always had been. The only one standing in her way was *her,* and deep down she understood that.

Once her mind was finally clear and relatively refocused, she slowly picked up the phone again, held it to her chest for long reflective moment, dialled the number and let the call connect.

"Hello?" a surprised voice asked.

"Hi, Mom, it's me," she whispered in a shaky voice.

"Hi, honey! Are you alright? You sound upset."

Her mothering tone was exactly what she needed to hear right now. It always seemed to instantly calm her. She breathed deeply trying to lighten up.

"I'm okay, just having a rough day, that's all."

"Oh honey, I'm sorry. I thought you were finally getting over Brett."

"No, Mom, it's not that. I just..." She took a long moment, trying to settle her emotions. "I need to ask you something."

"Okay."

"And I need you to be completely honest with me, okay? Can you do that?"

"This sounds serious, Bec. Is everything okay?"

She knew she was worrying her mom but didn't have a choice this time.

"I don't know... but I need your help."

"Of course, honey, you know I'm always here for you. What do you need to ask me?"

She paused for a moment, summoning the courage to ask the question.

"Was Dad the love of your life?"

Her mom was completely silent for a moment, obviously taken aback by the question. They rarely talked about her father, and hardly ever discussed the details of their relationship. It was usually too painful and too uncomfortable a subject for either of them.

She spoke softly. "Honestly... Yes, honey, he was. Why are you asking me this?"

Rebecca paused for a moment, trying to word the question as carefully as possible.

"Did you ever think... that he would hurt you the way he did?"

"Rebecca, that was a long time ago."

She could sense her mother's discomfort but wanted her answer more than anything.

"Did you? I need to know."

Her mother was silent for another long moment before finally answering.

"No. Honestly I never did. Your father was my whole world."

It was both the answer she expected and the answer she didn't want to hear.

"That's what I thought."

"Honey, why are you asking me this now? What's going on?"

"It's just something I've wondered for a very long time."

"Does this have something to do with Brett cheating on you?"

"Yes, but there's a lot more to it than that."

Rebecca's mom remained quiet for a little while. This particular conversation was both unexpected and a long time coming. For years they had subtly skirted the subject, neither of them eager to discuss the details, but it was clear now that Rebecca had questions.

"Rebecca, I know I haven't really talked much about the divorce, and that I usually avoid talking about it by focusing on the positive memories from our past, which was somewhat selfish on my part, but I need you to know some things about me and your father, okay?"

Stunned, Rebecca's senses instantly piqued as she gripped the phone. "Like what?"

Her mother took a long breath, collecting her thoughts.

"My life may not have worked out the way I'd planned with your father, but I don't for *one* minute regret the time we shared together, even now. And I'm not just saying that for your sake. He honestly *was* the love of my life.

"We met during our sophomore year in college, and he truly was the first man I'd ever fallen in love with. We had this *amazing* connection, and for years couldn't stand spending even the smallest amount of time apart. We were crazy in love, and those years were without a doubt the happiest of my life. It only got better when we had you and your brother.

"Losing him, losing that incredible love we shared together... What your father did to our family devastated me in a way I never knew possible and left me in a dark place for a long time. It took me years, but now when I look back on our time together, I try to focus on all of the good things because most of the years we spent together were happy ones.

"And despite the pain he put us through, I will *always* be thankful to him for giving me the two most amazing human beings on the planet."

A trace of a smile reached Rebecca's lips for the first time all day. "Thanks, Mom."

"It's true, Bec, and I'm so proud of the people you two have become. I like to think that you guys are the best part of both of us and that our love created who you are."

"Well, we had a pretty awesome mom raising us. Sometimes I wonder how you did it all." Even now it was difficult to give her dad half the credit.

"I always had you guys. I know I say it all the time, but I love you both more than you'll ever know. Our life wasn't perfect, but we always had each other, and that's all that matters. You will *always* be my highest priority and my greatest accomplishment."

Rebecca's mother's unconditional love and support always had a way of making even her darkest days brighter, and made her feel as if she could handle anything life threw at her. And today, it was exactly what she needed to hear.

"I love you too, Mom. You have no idea how much it means to me to know all of this. After everything you've been through, I honestly don't know how you can still see things the way you do... how you can still be such an optimist and believe in love."

Her mom paused, sighing in amusement. "It's because it's the best thing, the most *important* thing in life, Rebecca. It truly is. I know life doesn't come with guarantees, but sometimes you have to take a chance, have faith that love will find you, and be open to it when it does. I had it once and can appreciate how vital it is now more than ever. I truly hope you find it one day too."

As images of the previous day instantly flooded her mind, a warm feeling of contentment slowly filled her as an uncontrollable smile reached her lips.

"I think I already have."

"Oh honey... Was Brett the love of your life?"

"No, Mom, he wasn't."

# CHAPTER TEN

*Answers*

An equal mix of elation and trepidation filled Rebecca as she slowly hung up the phone.

In the nearly two years she had worked for the *Isthmus* she'd once called in sick when she was feeling perfectly fine. Brett had tried to talk her into it a handful of times, but ditching work was simply never something she felt comfortable doing.

After her eye-opening conversation with her mother the previous afternoon, followed by two liberal glasses of wine and a long evening of reflection, her priorities had decisively shifted.

With a newfound sense of resolution, she had finally determined what her next step would be. And she needed the day off from work to do it.

It was Monday, the day Azure had their largest delivery of the week, and Rebecca knew she could find Leo at the restaurant all morning helping the staff with inventory. Dropping in unannounced wasn't typically her style, but the importance and urgency of what she had planned took precedence and she knew Leo wouldn't mind at all.

State Street was already bustling with activity on another stunning spring day in Madison as Rebecca meandered her way through the early morning crowds toward the restaurant. As she approached the front door of Azure's modest façade, she could see two attractive young men cleaning the storefront windows while further inside a woman polished the floors with an industrial-style buffing machine. A tradition known as 'deep cleaning day,' started by Leo's father years ago, had become a weekly ritual that began each busy week.

On the surface Leo was a genuinely laid back person and didn't typically strike people as a control freak in the least, but when it came to the restaurant he was all business and left nothing to chance, especially on Monday mornings.

The weekly inventory routine was always a bit crazed, but it was also an enjoyable time to work. Leo usually let the music flow freely while he helped the day staff unload the delivery trucks and restock the kitchen shelves, refrigerators, and freezers while preparing the restaurant for the inevitable lunch rush. His staff actually preferred having him around, and always worked better with him there. He was excellent at managing people and they truly enjoyed his company.

As soon as one of the window washers recognized Rebecca, he stopped working, eagerly opened the door to let her inside, and greeted her with a flirtatious smile.

"Thanks. Is Leo around today?" she asked politely.

# Behind the Glass

"He sure is. I think I just heard him singing a few minutes ago in the back. Just follow the off-key voice." He winked at her and went back to cleaning.

She made her way through the spacious main dining room toward the kitchen, weaving her way through a sea of tables, when Leo burst through the swinging double doors laughing. He stopped in his tracks the moment he saw Rebecca, clearly surprised. His face instantly lit up.

"Hey, Bec! What brings *you* by so early? Shouldn't you be at work?"

His playful smile and positive energy was as infectious as always. Rebecca automatically smiled widely the moment she saw him.

"Hey, Leo! I'm actually playing hooky today."

" *You?* You're kidding! Is everything okay?" Leo teased.

"Yeah, everything's fine." Rebecca's smile faded. "Do you have a few minutes to talk?"

"For you, *always!*" Leo bellowed while subtly surveying the spaces of the restaurant. "Come on, we can talk in the side dining room. It's empty and probably the quietest spot in the restaurant right now." He shot her a quick familiar smile. "It's a little chaotic today, sorry."

He led her along the rear wall of the main dining room toward the bar area to a smaller, more intimate side one. It was the most flexible room in the restaurant and could be converted into a private dining room for larger parties anytime the need arose.

As Rebecca followed him she scanned the restaurant. Over a dozen of the staff were diligently engaged in various tasks, making the main dining room buzz with activity. Besides the deep cleaning, the glassware at the bar was being restocked from the previous night, light fixtures were being dusted, tablecloths and place settings were being neatly arranged at each table, and menus were being updated with the week's specials.

It immediately occurred to her that her timing wasn't exactly ideal.

"Oh, I'm sorry," she said under her breath as she followed Leo. "You're probably super busy right now. I can come back later if this is a bad time."

They stopped at a table in the side dining room and he pulled out a chair for her.

"I always have time for *you*. Seriously, Bec, you took time off work. It must be important and now you've got me curious. They can do without me for a little while, trust me." He gestured to her to sit down. "What's up?"

As she took her seat she briefly organized her thoughts, focusing on how she had planned this conversation in her mind last night.

"I need to ask you something."

"Okay." As Leo took his seat, his smile faded and his expression became more focused.

Behind the Glass

She paused, noticing the subtle protective concern in his eyes.

"This is probably going to seem a little strange coming from me, but in this case you are the *one* person I can count on to be completely honest with me."

"Honesty I can *always* do," he said, smiling again.

"I need some advice." She hesitated for a second as a sudden wave of nerves rose to the surface. "Um... I've gotten... *close* to someone recently, someone we both know. And every instinct I have is telling me it's probably the best thing in the world and that I would be crazy not to get closer to this person. But the overly cautious, untrusting part of me is afraid of getting hurt again. Leo, you know me better than anyone and I value your opinion so much."

"You're talking about Michael, aren't you?" Leo interrupted.

She could always depend on Leo's sharp perception.

"Yes."

He paused for a long moment, locking eyes with her intently before he spoke, "He's in love with you, Rebecca."

She stared back at him stunned and speechless.

"I could see it a mile away the night I introduced you at the dance club."

"You could?" She furrowed her brow and looked away for a moment, thinking back to that night. "That actually wasn't the first time we'd met."

"I know." Leo shot her a knowing smile.

"He told you?"

"He didn't have to. It wasn't too hard to figure out."

She was at a loss for words for a moment.

"You never said anything."

He shrugged his shoulders. "You were with Brett."

She looked puzzled, trying to put it all together.

"How do you know he's in love with me?"

He smiled, shaking his head in wonder.

"Haven't you seen the way he looks at you? The way he looks after you? You don't always seem to notice things like that, but I did."

She smiled involuntarily, surprised by Leo's observations.

"You did?"

Seeming almost amused at her reaction, he leaned in as he spoke.

"At the dance club, at Claire's house, at my wedding... Yeah, I did."

"I had no idea that you knew."

"Who do you think gave him your address?" He smiled widely.

She smiled, laughing lightly under her breath. "Oh, that's right."

"Right after you and Brett split up, he was really worried about you. He tried to hide it, but I could tell how he felt about you. He told me what he had done for you on our wedding night, giving you a place to stay, and I'm grateful to him for that. He and I talked a lot during those weeks and... I don't know, I just *knew*. He just seemed to notice things about you, seemed to know you a lot better than I had realized." He paused, looking down momentarily. "I also knew then that I had set you up with the wrong person in the first place."

"Leo..." She hated the idea of Leo blaming himself again.

"No, Bec, I should have known. Brett's been one of my best friends for a long time and deep down he really is a good person, but he wasn't right for you, and I should have known better. I wish I could tell you that what he did to you surprised me, but it didn't."

"What are you saying?"

"After we graduated, he told me how he wanted to stop dating and settle down with one person. For the first time, he seemed to really mean it and after he'd been single for a while I really believed him. I was hesitant to set you up with him at first, but when I saw you together, I don't know, it felt right. It was a side of him I'd never seen before. He fell *hard*, Rebecca."

"I had no idea."

A sudden rush of suppressed feelings toward Brett sprang to the surface at once.

"For a while he was a different guy than the Brett I'd known in college. Because of you. I think you actually made him want to be a better person."

"It's still not your fault, you know."

"I know. I still feel responsible though. I had hoped he'd changed, but I guess old habits die hard. You were just the last person in the world I wanted to see hurt."

"Trust me, I have absolutely no doubt of that, but I'm okay now, *really*. You have to stop blaming yourself for what he did. I've moved on."

"Have you?"

She looked down briefly, knowing exactly what Leo was getting at.

"I thought I had. But the last few days... I don't know, I just feel... *lost*. And I'm not sure how to fix it."

"You're not lost, Bec. It may feel that way, but you're not. You should give yourself more credit. You just need to know Brett's side of it."

Amazingly Leo always seemed to know exactly what she was thinking, even if it was subconsciously. He'd been doing it since they were kids. He was more perceptive than most people gave him credit for, and she could always depend on him to put everything into perspective.

And he was right; she *did* want to know Brett's side of what had happened between them and what had led him to do what he did. She needed answers.

"Well, I don't think talking to him now is such a good idea. Besides, he probably knows better than to cross *you*." She shot him a teasing smile.

# Behind the Glass

Leo shrugged his shoulders guiltily. "I *may* have given him the distinct impression that I would literally break his legs if he ever went near you again."

Rebecca's eyes widened. "You didn't."

"I'm sorry, Bec, but he broke your heart *at my wedding*. I was pretty pissed off at the time. He crossed a pretty big line."

"I see."

Leo's temper never ceased to amaze her, especially where she was concerned.

"Anyway, he's been pretty hesitant to contact you because of that."

She raised her brow, smiling. "Can you blame him?"

"No, but I know he's wanted to see you."

"Yeah, I know."

"You do?"

"He actually called me a couple weeks ago. He didn't leave a message but I saw it was him on the caller I.D."

"He wants to talk to you, to find a way to apologize. Despite what he did, it's killing him that he hurt you."

"Have you talked to him?"

"Yeah, I have. He stopped by the restaurant last week and we talked for a while. He gave me a letter to give to you, and left it up to me to decide when you were ready to read it."

"A *letter*?"

Rebecca was stunned. A letter from Brett was completely unexpected.

"I think you should read it, Bec. I never thought I'd be saying this, but you need to hear what he has to say. You're never going to get past this and be able to move on until you do."

As she looked back at Leo, Rebecca felt deeply touched and extremely grateful knowing how much he'd always cared for her. Their lifelong bond was something she would never take for granted, and she knew he'd always have her back no matter what.

She reached out and squeezed his hand. "Thanks, Leo."

His expression became more serious, holding her gaze intently.

"Listen to me." His voice was calm and reassuring. "Your dad cheated on your mom, left you guys, and really never looked back. Your mom shut down and in her own way, never looked back either. Brett cheated on you and I can't imagine what that felt like. Bad things happen, Rebecca. But good things happen too. Look at Isabel. I knew she was the person I wanted to spend the rest of my life with the first time I met her. I can't imagine my life without her and every day with her just gets better. You deserve that too. More than you know. You asked for my advice and I'm telling you, *with absolute certainty,* to trust your instincts."

Leo had always had a way of simplifying everything and cutting through to the truth. He had confirmed what she had known all along, but for some reason it didn't seem entirely real until she heard it from him.

She breathed a sigh of relief. This is what she had come for.

He briefly excused himself to retrieve Brett's letter from his office, returning minutes later. As he handed it to her, he held her gaze for a long moment, smiling sincerely. "I hope this gives you the answers you're looking for."

"Thanks, Leo. For everything. I don't know what I'd do without you sometimes."

"Hey, you're family to me, Bec, and you always will be. I'll *always* be here for you."

He gave her a long tight hug before walking her to the front door. As they parted, she slowly began feeling more at peace. She tucked the letter into her purse and began strolling down State Street reflecting on their discussion.

As her scattered thoughts recalled each detail, she found herself smiling thinking of how Leo had known about Michael's feelings for her all this time yet never said a thing.

She replayed memories of Michael in her mind, wondering who else had picked up how attracted they were to each other. She had always assumed their intense connection had been mostly in her mind, but obviously it had been more apparent to everyone else than she realized.

And more importantly, it must have been apparent to Brett.

Her gait slowed as her heart slowly sank, imagining the past months from Brett's perspective. She wondered how transparent she had been during their relationship, and if her behaviour was what drove him into the arms of another woman. Latent feelings of guilt and remorse filled her as she eventually came to a halt amidst the busy morning hustle.

A sudden, urgent need to read his letter grew stronger by the minute.

As someone brushed past her, knocking lightly into her shoulder, she came back to the present and quickly became aware of where she was ironically standing. The sleek inviting storefront of Behind the Glass stood before her, beckoning her to come inside.

She found it fitting that fate would lead her here, back to where it all began.

Without a second thought, she opened the door, instantly absorbing the rich smells of coffee and baked goods. As the door slowly closed behind her, the quiet calm of her oasis embraced her like an old friend. Memories of late nights filled her mind as she slowly made her way to the back to order her favourite latte. The shop felt different somehow, probably because she'd never been there this early in the morning, yet it felt completely familiar and soothing.

# Behind the Glass

As she glanced toward the staircase, she recalled Michael's beautiful painting and how she felt the first time she connected with it. It was such a strong connection, yet it seemed like a lifetime ago. Now, the walls were overflowing with her artwork, just as she'd always imagined.

She scanned the shop for Grace and Ethan, but they were nowhere to be found. After she ordered her coffee, she quietly asked the young girl behind the counter if they were in the back. She shook her head no, saying they had taken a personal day and would be back tomorrow.

As enjoyable as it would have been to say hello, she was actually grateful for anonymity at the moment. She was going to need uninterrupted privacy to read Brett's letter, and was relieved to find the second floor reading area mostly uninhabited.

Fittingly, her favourite lush reading chair was ready and waiting for her.

She took the letter out of her purse, sipped her coffee, and took a long deep breath before reading it. Brett had never been one to write her letters in the past, and she really didn't know what to expect. She was anxious and completely intrigued by the answers she'd hoped to find.

And equally nervous about the questions it may leave her with.

*Dear Rebecca,*

*If you're reading this, it means that Leo is taking a huge leap of faith and feels that you're ready to let me offer you the only thing I can at this point – an explanation. I owe you that and I hope you'll read this letter knowing how much I wish I could tell you all of this in person, but I know that's not possible right now. Please just know that I think about you all the time and can only imagine how much I've hurt you. I would give anything to change that.*

*Whether you realize it or not, you have changed me forever. No matter what happens next, I will never be the man I was before I met you. I had no idea the impact you would have on my life, on me, when we first met, but I know now that there's no going back.*

*I honestly had never met anyone like you before, and frankly had never had a relationship so deep or so close with anyone. I'll admit that I'd never been one to want to settle down with one person, especially in college, because I was always more interested in having fun and exploring my options. At least that was the lie I decided to tell myself for years. The truth is, I never wanted to let anyone into my life long enough to decide they didn't want to be with me. It just seemed easier to be the first to leave before the other person had the chance. As absurd as that logic was, it was all I'd known until I met you. You changed all of that for me.*

*The night Leo introduced us was, for lack of a better word, surreal. You were undeniably the most* amazing, beautiful, kind, sexy, funny, intelligent woman I'd ever met and I knew immediately that I wanted to do whatever I could to be with you. For the first time in my life, I was totally out of my element and completely unprepared.

I always felt like the luckiest man in the world to be with someone like you, and although I never showed it, deep down I knew you were completely out of my league. I know there were times during our relationship that you felt we were moving too fast, or that I wanted too much from you, but the truth was I didn't want you to leave me. I suppose we all have our insecurities and that was mine – losing you.

I slowly realized we didn't always see eye to eye on everything, and that you are a very guarded person by nature, but I couldn't help feeling that you were slowly pulling away from me little by little over the time we were together. I tried doing everything I could think of to improve our relationship by spending more time together and suggesting moving in together, but you weren't ready for that. In time I had hoped that you would open up to me more, but you never felt comfortable enough to let me in entirely.

For a while I wondered if there was someone else, and I found myself doubting your feelings for me. As my imagination and insecurities gradually got the better of me, mixed with too much alcohol at the wedding, I did something I swore I'd never do to you. If I could go back in time and take that moment back,

*I would. A million times over. You didn't deserve that.*

*Seeing the hurt in your eyes in that moment changed me permanently. I knew then it was the end for us, and there was nothing I could do or say to fix it. And I was completely to blame. It was in that moment that I realized how much I truly loved you, as bizarre as that sounds.*

*Rebecca, you were the woman I wanted to build a life with, the woman I wanted to marry and have children with, the woman I wanted to grow old with and love forever. You were the one. And I wanted to build my entire world around you. I'd never felt that way about anyone before and may never again.*

*All the years I'd spent 'having fun and exploring my options' seem completely wasted now. Until I'd met you, I had honestly never understood people like Leo and Isabel who wanted to be with only each other for the rest of their lives. Now I can't imagine anything else.*

*And despite everything, I still love you. More than you can imagine.*

*After talking with Leo, I know that what I did has changed you and that you're in a very different place now, but there will always be a part of me that hopes you'd be willing to talk to me again. I know I have no right to ask anything of you, but at this point I'll take anything you're willing to give, and will respect your decision if you never want to see me again.*

*Above all, I want you to be happy.*

# Behind the Glass

*You are simply the most amazing person I've ever met, and you deserve to be with someone who will never hurt you and will love you more than anything in this world, forever.*

*As for me, I'll always be thankful to you for opening my mind and my heart to love and making me realize what's most important in life.*

*More than words can ever express, you truly have changed me forever.*

*Always yours,*

*Brett*

As Rebecca slowly lowered the letter to her lap, staring out across the upper floor of the shop in a daze, she was both numb and overcome with emotion at the same time. The honesty of Brett's letter astonished her, and she was touched deeply by what it must have taken to write it.

Distant memories and suppressed emotions drifted back to the surface, as she reflected on his words while taking her time to let it all sink in. She found herself reading the letter again and again in wonder.

It was clear to her now that she had never truly known the extent of his feelings for her during their time together. He had told her countless times that he loved her, and had always seemed completely enamoured with her, but he'd never expressed the feelings on the pages before her until now. It was a revelation.

As she read his words, she slowly realized how her actions, though subtle, had impacted him so deeply. As much as she hated to acknowledge it, she simply wasn't as invested in the relationship as she should have been. Certainly not as much as he had been.

She may not have actually cheated on Brett, but she effectively pushed him away at every turn. She kept him at a safe distance when he tried to get closer, and despite his constant efforts to break through, she never let herself share her true feelings with him.

And she was in love with someone else. Undeniably.

Her actions didn't excuse what he did, but she wasn't innocent either. She had been content to blame Brett for ruining their relationship, but she had played her part too and that wasn't fair to him. After finally hearing everything from his perspective, she realized that he was merely a man in love with someone who was emotionally unavailable, and in a moment of clouded ambivalence, had made a huge mistake due to his own insecurities.

Though painful, it was simply *one* mistake, one moment that changed everything.

Brett didn't have an affair with another woman for months on end during his fifteen-year marriage. He didn't get that woman pregnant and divorce his wife and two kids to start a new life with his new family without looking back.

# Behind the Glass

Brett was *not* her father and shouldn't be compared to him.

For the first time in her life she was able to clearly see how entirely different her family's circumstances were to anything or anyone else in her life. Although the familiar emotions and associated pain may have felt exactly the same, it was misguided to liken these two men, these two completely different relationships to each other. It was also foolish and short sighted of her to fear future relationships, to fear *love* because of either one of them. Every situation is different and as her mother had said, life doesn't come with guarantees.

After reading Brett's letter, talking with Leo this morning, and talking with her mother yesterday, she was ultimately filled with more peace and clarity than she had ever felt in her life. It was remarkable how the past twenty-four hours had brought such an eye opening epiphany to light, and now suddenly, everything finally clicked.

With a new sense of confidence and determination, she carefully folded the letter and placed it in her purse as she stood up. She took a long look around her cherished bookstore café and felt comforted by the fact that it had always been there for her. Over the past months it had been a place to hide, a place to discover, a place to shine, and a place to fall in love.

She didn't know what the future held with Michael, but she knew she would never find out if she didn't let him break through her walls.

It was time to stop hiding. From herself, from her past, from the things that may break her, and find out what the future would hold.

It was time to come out from behind the glass.

# CHAPTER ELEVEN

*Home*

When Rebecca was in college she would occasionally awaken to the most bizarre and heart-racing dreams of her life. The details were rarely the same, but the feelings they instilled when she awoke stayed with her for a long time. They typically found her in everyday scenarios racing against time, either trying to get to a class clear across campus or finishing a complex assignment on time. They invariably ended with her desperately trying to do something or get somewhere before it was too late. She constantly found herself running and running, but never making it in time. She would jolt out of her dreams in a complete panic with her heart pounding, and it would take most of the morning to calm down. Whatever she had wanted or was trying to achieve was relentlessly *just* out of her reach.

Those unshakable familiar feelings were now coming back in full force.

As she drove along the winding roads through the rolling hills of Wisconsin's sprawling farmland, she found it difficult to keep to a respectable speed. The urgent, irrepressible need to get back to Vale Ranch, back to Michael, as quickly as possible, was steadily consuming her.

With each passing mile, her emotions wavered back and forth. One minute she welled with excitement and felt completely confident at knowing for the first time in her life exactly what she wanted, and the next minute her heart sank with panic and uncertainty that she had made a serious mistake and that it was too late.

Unable to shake the lingering cloud of regret, she replayed their last encounter in her mind over and over. Endless images of their day at the ranch together, the way he held her in his arms in his secret backyard, the way he looked after her all day long, that life altering kiss ... and the way she had pushed him away, whirled around in her head in a frenzy during what felt like the longest forty minute ride of her life. Looking back on the events of that day with such newfound clarity made her realize what a fool she'd been all along.

Despite the trepidation she'd felt up until now about being with him, driven by her own insecurities and failed relationships, she finally recognized that he had never once given her any reason to doubt him, not ever. From that very first night, he had done nothing but prove to her over and over what kind of person he was and how he felt about her.

Michael had been straightforward and honest the first night they'd met, and had openly admitted that he wanted to know more about her. And then she left him without an explanation, only telling him her name. When they met again at the dance club, he

# Behind the Glass

was discreet about their previous encounter, and respected the fact that she had a boyfriend, vowing to leave her alone.

Weeks later at Claire's house, despite how much he undoubtedly wanted to be with her, he stopped himself and tried to ease *her* pain when she told him she couldn't be. Accepting the difficult position she was in, he willingly sacrificed his own happiness, putting her needs first.

And then at the wedding, he did something for her that she now realized defined his character more than anything else. In her lowest, most heartbroken moment, he rescued her – in more ways than he would ever know. He took care of her when she needed it the most, putting his own feelings aside, and only thinking of what *she* needed that night. Talking for hours together washed away her sadness, and brought to life a new friendship that would only grow in the weeks to come.

He gave her space when she needed it, and was incredibly patient with her over those next weeks, never giving up on her for one second. The gallery opening surprise was one of the most thoughtful, touching gestures anyone had ever done for her, and it made her happier than she could have imagined.

And he never asked for a thing in return, apart from her friendship.

As their relationship grew, she was continually astounded at how kind-hearted he was and how lucky she was having him in her life. And she trusted him completely.

The day they spent together at the ranch was nothing shy of perfect. Despite how strong his feelings were for her, he planned their day together carefully and took things slowly, letting her set the pace. When she opened up to him, he didn't push her for information or question her character, he simply listened without judgment and with unconditional acceptance.

And he promised her, unequivocally, that he would never hurt her, ever.

Still, she couldn't shake the overwhelming feeling of dismay that pushing him away at such a pivotal point may have been more than he could take. Leaving him *again* without an explanation and staying away without so much as one word seemed cruel. He didn't deserve that. After everything he had done for her, after how selfless he had always been, was that rejection enough to change everything? Honestly, she wasn't sure.

She flashed back to his last words to her: *"I'm here, okay. I'm not going anywhere."*

As she turned off the main road onto the long gravel driveway and passed under the massive wooden Vale Ranch sign overhead, she took a deep breath and hoped with every fibre of her being that she wasn't too late, that he hadn't gone anywhere, and hadn't given up her.

# Behind the Glass

She may have felt lost at times, and been an emotional work in progress since the day they'd met, but now, at this very moment, she finally felt as if she was on the same page as him.

More than anything in the world she wanted to continue their story *together.*

As she pulled into the parking area, the ranch bustled with activity. Groups of campers dressed in equestrian gear walked along the paths to the stables, while camp counsellors led group instructions in the riding rings and throughout the lodges. Memories of her time at the ranch flashed in her mind and filled her with anticipation. She couldn't be sure if what she was feeling stemmed from childhood memories or from thoughts of Michael. Either way, her heart began to race in a familiar way with each step toward the main lodge.

Just before she reached the base of the main staircase of Sawyer Lodge, a familiar voice called out from behind her.

"Rebecca?"

She turned and in the distance spotted Grace with a group of middle school-aged girls near one of the bunk houses. Grace waved and broke away from the group the moment their eyes met.

Rebecca smiled and waved back, but Grace didn't return the smile. Her usual animated persona was visibly masked with serious concern. The look in

Grace's eyes spoke volumes and made Rebecca's heart sink instantly. This was not a good sign.

"Hi, Grace." Her voice wavered slightly as nerves began to build.

As Grace reached her, she glanced around the property and lightly took Rebecca's arm.

"Hi, hon, it's good to see you. Can we talk somewhere privately?"

She was as straightforward as always, but also warm and sincere.

"Um... sure."

Without a word, Grace quietly led her up the stairs of Sawyer Lodge into the main gathering hall. The space inside was enormous and rustically beautiful. The open double-height living/dining area was a barnlike room crowned by well-worn beams above, anchored by a floor to ceiling stone fireplace in the center of the room, and graced by a span of tall windows that overlooked the acres of rolling hills of Vale Ranch.

Rebecca took a brief moment to absorb the lodge as a mass of adolescent memories of her time at the ranch rushed to the forefront of her mind. The smells, the sounds, the very feel of it hadn't changed a bit over the years. Though she had only spent one weekend there at age eleven, she somehow felt as if she'd come home again. She smiled automatically.

"Right over here, hon. This is one of my favourite little nooks."

# Behind the Glass

Tucked away, just off the main room, was a quaint secluded window seat just large enough for two, overlooking the eastern edge of the property. As they settled in, Rebecca gazed out the window at the stables, remembering how she and Michael had strolled along the paths together. As her heart skipped a beat, the need to be with him again was stronger than ever.

Grace focused on Rebecca and smiled warmly before she spoke.

"I told him to trust my instincts. They are rarely *ever* wrong."

"Trust your instincts?"

Grace had a habit of expressing herself without preface. Michael had described it once and had always found it both amusing and confusing at the same time. Rebecca now understood what he had been talking about.

"About you." She paused, looking at her pointedly. "I knew you were going to be the one to change his life. From the moment you started coming into our little shop, I sensed that there was something special about you. It was just a feeling, an instinct, but as each week passed I became more certain that you were the one he'd been waiting for, the one he'd been *searching* for his whole life. It may sound crazy, but I just knew."

Grace paused and gently placed her hand on Rebecca's. "Just like I knew that when you were ready, you'd come back."

Rebecca smiled. "No, it's not crazy. You have good instincts."

"When it comes to Michael, yes I usually do."

Rebecca recalled the many conversations she'd had with Michael about Grace and how she had always looked out for him in her own way. At times she seemed to know him better than he knew himself. Grace and Leo were similar in that way. Rebecca had always trusted Leo's judgment completely, just as Michael had always trusted Grace's. An indescribable comfort comes from knowing that your closest confidants will always be there for you no matter what.

"Grace, I may never understand how or why our paths crossed at your little shop, but I have to believe it was for a reason. You say that you knew that I would be the one to change his life, but you should know that *he* has changed *my* life in more ways than I could ever describe. I'm only now really appreciating how much."

Rebecca looked down for a moment as the harrowing cloud of regret drifted back to her.

"I'm just glad you're here, hon. Not only to prove me right," Grace paused with a playful smirk, "but because he needs to know that he didn't ruin everything with you."

"He thinks *he* ruined everything?" Her heart sank.

"Of course he does. He's been so quiet the past couple days, even with me, but I've broken through a little and I think he feels as if he's scared you away. He doesn't know how to make it right and he's been... isolated. "

"Isolated?"

Noticing the concern in Rebecca's eyes, Grace gave her a reassuring look.

"Since we were kids, when either of us needed some space we would saddle up one of our favourite horses and ride out across the ranch to the edge of the property to get away from everything. During my rebellious years, I probably spent more time out there than anywhere else, but I always found the answers I was looking for." She paused, looking out the window toward the majestic landscape below. "Clarity can often be found in the most beautiful things in nature. This place has a way of grounding you, trust me."

Rebecca smiled softly, remembering the peaceful feeling that washed over her each time she came back to this place. "I know what you mean."

Grace gazed out toward the forest on the ridge past the rolling hills before them.

"He took Duke out at dawn and I haven't seen him since."

"I bet I can guess where he is."

Grace nodded. "And you'd be right. Our backyard is about as isolated as you can get."

"Isolated... and *safe*. I get it, trust me."

They both certainly shared the need for a hideout from time to time. Only now she wished she was with him in his secret backyard instead of being his reason for hiding.

"You do, don't you? You really understand him."

"I do. More than I realize sometimes."

"Well, you're probably the first."

"The first what?"

"You're the first woman to really see him for who he truly is on the inside. Most women, at least the very few he's been with, only see the stunningly handsome exterior and stop there. He's just not your typical good-looking, rugged cowboy. He's so much more complex than that."

The memory of Claire's shameless pursuit of him suddenly flashed in her mind.

"He is. He's unlike anyone I've ever known." Rebecca paused, taking her time to reflect before going on. "He's kind, honest, intelligent, funny, generous, and probably one of the most honourable, moral people I've ever known. He stays true to himself. It's what I love about him."

Grace's face steadily lit up more and more with each word as she listened.

"He's all of those things and more. Of course I've known him my whole life, so I'm a bit biased, but he's an exceptional man. I would do anything for him, and I can't tell you how much his happiness means to me. Since meeting you, I've seen distinct changes in him, and I can honestly say the impact you've had on him has been remarkable. No one has ever been so completely in sync with him. He's waited a long time to find you."

She gently placed her hand on Rebecca's again. "And Rebecca... he is just *so* completely, irrevocably in love with you, hon, you really have no idea."

Taken aback at hearing the words aloud, Rebecca was speechless for a moment.

Grace looked out the window again and pointed to an innocuous looking barn structure on the eastern edge of the property below. "Do you see that building down there?"

Rebecca spotted it and nodded.

"That's Michael's artist's loft. It's where he works and lives. Since meeting you he has been spending a lot more time there, and has been painting more than ever lately. You definitely bring out his creative side. Is it safe to assume he hasn't shown it to you yet?"

"Um... no, he hasn't. We didn't walk over that way when I was here. We headed straight to the stables before our ride."

"Not surprising." Grace quickly stood up and took Rebecca's hand. "Come with me."

Without another word, Grace led Rebecca away from the window seat nook, out of the main lodge, down the main staircase, and onto a path leading to Michael's loft. The whole walk was a complete blur. Grace seemed as determined as ever, while Rebecca followed without the slightest objection.

She was thoroughly filled with wonder as they approached the barn-style building that in no way indicated that it housed an artist's studio, let alone a residence of any kind.

Michael had given her a fairly extensive tour of the ranch, showing her all of his favourite places, yet he never took her to his loft. He never even alluded to it in any way. She hadn't given it a second thought until now, but it seemed completely uncharacteristic, and she couldn't imagine why he would have kept it from her. Grace didn't seem surprised by this at all, which only fuelled her curiosity more.

As they reached the front door to the loft, Grace eventually slowed her gait and turned around to face her. She took both of Rebecca's hands in hers for a long moment and gave her the warmest, most contented smile.

"I'm taking a big chance here, and frankly I don't exactly have Michael's blessing to do this, but every instinct I have is pointing me in this direction."

"You don't have his blessing to do what?"

Grace glanced back toward the loft and back to Rebecca.

"You need to see what's behind this door. You need to understand that *you* are the one who's changed *his* life. Rebecca, you need to see what true love looks like. His love."

"I don't understand. What's behind this door?"

Utterly intrigued, she tried to make sense of what Grace was talking about.

"That's for you alone, my dear."

# Behind the Glass

Grace stepped away slowly, gently releasing her hands, and began making her way back down the stone path toward the lodge.

"Wait, where are you going?"

"Oh, I'll be around, hon, don't worry," she said, still slowly walking backward. "This is just something you need to see by yourself. Trust me on this, okay?"

Still unsure of what to expect, Rebecca agreed. "Okay ..."

Sensing her hesitation, Grace paused and focused on Rebecca with complete confidence. "Take your time Rebecca. Just follow your heart. I promise it won't lead you astray."

Grace smiled contently and happily made her way back to another small group of teenage girls, hugging each one warmly as if joining in on an overdue reunion, her sheer zeal for life rubbing off on all who crossed her path. She was definitely one of a kind.

Looking back at the loft, Rebecca stood motionless for a long time while quietly summoning the nerve to open the door and reveal what Grace seemed to think she needed to see, and what Michael had mysteriously concealed.

Grace's words repeated endlessly in her mind as she slowly reached for the door handle.

*You need to see what true love looks like. His love.*

She stepped inside the room with her eyes closed, shutting the door behind her. She leaned against the back of the door for a long moment, soaking in the peaceful silence while taking a long deep breath before opening her eyes. The smell of him was everywhere, mixed with the faint aroma of oil paints and pastels, and the subtle scent of the wooden barn.

As she slowly opened her eyes, what stood before her was astounding.

The mid-day sunlight bathed the room brilliantly in an almost angelic aura. The immense open space and high wooden beams overhead glowed softly, while the rustic dark hardwood floors anchored the space perfectly. The understated décor was the ideal backdrop for the most breath-taking and unexpected works of art she'd ever laid her eyes on. It was stunning.

As she slowly made her way to the center of the room, she found herself surrounded in virtually every direction by dozens upon dozens of paintings, drawings, and sketches in every conceivable media, all flawlessly created by Michael.

Each piece varied vastly in style, size, shape, colour, texture, and level of detail, yet they all possessed a similar character as a uniform body of work. Every exquisite painting, every sketch, every single work of art in this incredible room, also shared one singular trait: the subject matter.

To her utter amazement, every single one... was of *her.*

Astonished, she whirled slowly in the center of the room as her heart pounded, absorbing each image. He had elegantly captured countless moments and emotions over the past several months, all entirely from his memory of her. It was simply incredible.

A small black and white charcoal sketch depicted her curled up in her reading chair with her nose buried in one of her favourite novels. A larger, vividly coloured acrylic painting on canvas portrayed her walking down the aisle in her dark navy bridesmaid dress holding white lilies. A somewhat abstract muted watercolour showed only her sleeping face bathed in candlelight.

The level of detail and accuracy was beyond compare, and the meticulous care he took with each one was obvious. As she slowly examined each work of art, she was overcome with emotion as she finally came to understand that *she* was his muse.

Lost in this surreal moment of revelation, she realized that she had truly never known feelings this powerful before. It was exhilarating. She hugged her arms tightly around herself to calm the gentle trembling that was slowly building inside of her. Soaking in each beautiful image, she quietly fought back unexpected tears of joy brimming in her eyes.

For the first time since they had met she was finally able to see herself through *his* eyes and truly know beyond a doubt how much he loved her.

Grace had been right all along. This room was the embodiment of love. His love.

This amazing man with whom she had fallen deeply in love had created the most romantic, extraordinary, and awe-inspiring art gallery she could have ever imagined.

And it was the most beautiful thing she had ever seen.

Captivated by his artwork just as she had been on that first night by the painting by the stairs, time and space seemed to gradually fade away. His striking artwork drew her in with a unique yet familiar character that was raw with emotion. Taking her time, she lovingly surveyed each breath-taking piece that surrounded her, slowly turning toward the door only to find Michael standing in the doorway, staring at her.

Frozen, she could feel her face begin to flush as her heart raced.

She had no idea how long he had been there, but based on his intense expression, long enough to take in her reaction to his private gallery. She noticed an underlying vulnerability in his eyes that she had never seen before. As they both stood motionless, she felt as if she had just exposed a personal visual diary of sorts, revealing all of his deepest most private feelings.

In this moment, to her surprise, it was *she* who was breaking down all of his boundaries.

They both remained speechless, locking eyes together as time stood still.

"You came back," he finally said quietly.

She smiled instantly at hearing his voice.

"Of course I came back." She paused, finding her voice. "You knew I would."

His expression remained serious as he spoke softly.

"I did, but... What's changed in just two days?"

"Everything."

His brow furrowed with curiosity, yet he said nothing.

"It may be hard to believe, but yes... *everything*."

The last two days flashed in her mind in a blur... leaving him, sobbing in her car, hiding from everything, talking with her mom, talking with Leo, reading Brett's letter, coming here, talking with Grace, seeing this amazing collection he had created... so many moments leading to this one.

"It's been an enlightening two days."

His expression softened slightly, but he remained silent, allowing her to continue.

"I had a moment of clarity today and it was the first time in my life that I've felt like everything finally came into focus at once. It was as if I was looking through my camera lens and in one singular moment, I could see the world clearly and suddenly it all made sense.

"I realized that I've spent my whole life being careful, never taking any risks, or making the wrong decisions. Always being the good girl. For as long as I can remember, I've always only listened to my head instead of my heart, fooling myself into thinking it was the smart thing to do. The *safe* thing to do. And where has that gotten me?

"Since I met you, I've slowly lost that control. My feelings for you were unlike anything I'd known before and it scared me to death. I've always felt completely vulnerable around you, because you've always only seen me for who I really am, and known what I truly feel and think. That kind of honestly between two people was amazing and terrifying for me all at once. Letting you in, letting you break through... was *overwhelming*. My first instinct was to run because running has always been the only way I knew to protect myself from getting hurt."

She paused as a flash of mixed emotions filled her at once, then she focused on him, on his beautiful soulful eyes with complete confidence in her voice.

"But I don't want to run anymore... to *hide* anymore. For the first time in my life, I can honestly say that I'm not scared."

He looked at her in awe. "You're not?"

"No. Not at all." She smiled softly. "And do you know why?"

He subtly shook his head. "Why?"

"Because of you." She paused, looking deeply into his eyes as she spoke slowly. "You see, I'm still up on that ledge about to jump, but now I know I won't fall. I can't. Because you're up there with me. Holding my hand. And I know you'll never let me fall. You never have."

She paused, fighting back unexpected tears.

## Behind the Glass

"So, of course I came back. I know it's taken me far too long. But I know now with absolute certainty... that *this* is where I belong. With you. I love you, Michael."

# CHAPTER TWELVE

*Love*

Hearing those three words for the first time left Michael speechless. He was in a daze just looking into those beautiful green eyes again, still slowly processing everything she had said. Rebecca stood motionless with the mid-day sunlight at her back, glowing radiantly with her eyes still fixed on him. Filled with a newfound confidence deep inside her that drew him in completely, this was definitely not the same woman from two days ago.

To his bemusement, everything *had* changed.

All of the doubt and inner turmoil he'd put himself through over the past two days gradually dissolved with each word that washed over him. The details of their time apart, and what led her back here with such certainty, were a mystery to him but honestly, it didn't matter in that moment. All that mattered was that she loved him.

Seeing her here in this place, in his personal artistic refuge, surrounded by everything he had created over the past several months was entirely unexpected, yet somehow fitting. He had been struggling for weeks with how to introduce her to this place without overwhelming her, and ironically, he knew immediately who had led her here the moment he opened the door. Grace always had her subtle ways of giving them the push they needed.

# Behind the Glass

Without a word, he slowly stepped inside the room, closing the door behind him as he held her unwavering gaze. Neither said a word for what felt like an eternity, yet their eyes conveyed a silent conversation deep within their souls as they gradually drew closer to one another in the center of the room. Fitting together like the final two pieces of an intricate puzzle that took months to complete, they both finally felt like they had come home.

He stood over her for a moment just inches away, lightly brushing his hand across her cheek while savouring her exquisite beauty in this moment before leaning in. He hesitated before kissing her, purely out of instinct, but she was already moving in toward him with a newfound determination. That familiar look of pure, shameless desire instantly pulled him by his core as he brazenly took her face in his hands, kissing her even more deeply than he had in the stables after their ride. The intensity they both felt the moment their lips met was unparalleled, only this time she returned the kiss with more passion and wanting than he could have ever imagined.

Giving in to her every yearning, every longing, every buried feeling she'd ever felt for him since the day they had met, she slid her arms around his neck, pressing her body against his while running her fingers through his hair. Savouring the taste of her lips on his and breathing in her wonderful scent, he pulled her closer to him, slowly sliding one hand down her back while the other hand found its way through her hair toward the base of her neck.

Overcome with an intense need for him that she had never experienced before, every nerve ending came alive at once everywhere he touched her. Her body melted into him as her blood ran hot through her veins. The intimate connection she felt with him, and the absolute trust they shared opened her heart and soul in a way she never knew possible before now.

With every kiss, every touch, every breath, she could feel herself letting go... letting the walls slip away forever... allowing him to see her as no one ever had before. Giving herself to him completely and opening herself to his extraordinary love was the most liberating, and quite possibly most sensual experience of her life.

She belonged to him now, unequivocally.

With her heart racing and her skin positively tingling, she slowly ran her hands down the sides of his neck, over the collar of his shirt, and slowly down his lean sculpted chest. Sensing an intense shift of emotion deep within her, his hands made their way down to the small of her back as his embrace became noticeably stronger. He was impetuously under her spell.

She gingerly ran her fingers along the edges of his button-down shirt, gently tracing each button with her fingers as she went. When she reached the top one she slowly undid it and steadily moved down to the next one. Surprising himself, he interrupted her, taking her hands in his while catching his breath before he spoke.

"Are you sure?" He gently touched his forehead to hers, still breathless.

"I've never been so sure of anything in my life," she breathed, kissing him again.

Pulling her toward him while subtly walking backward, he slowly led her by the hand to a staircase nestled into one side of the room leading to a loft bedroom. She followed without hesitation as a fire slowly began to build deep inside of her with each step she took.

As they reached the quaint bedroom that overlooked the studio below, she was struck by its humble décor that reflected his personality perfectly. Anchored by a custom built floor-to-ceiling wooden bookcase surrounding a tall picture window along the back wall, the cosy space only contained a large rustic-looking dresser, a night stand, and a simple Shaker-style bed.

Unlike the studio space below, only two pieces of artwork graced its walls. A striking abstract acrylic painting of a galloping horse hung on the wall opposite the bed, and a single framed photograph of State Street at night, one of hers, hung directly over his bed.

Her heart skipped a beat the moment she recognized it.

"It reminds me of the night we met." He smiled, seeming to read her mind.

She smiled back, remembering that night vividly, as he gently took her in his arms again, delicately tracing his finger along her beautiful face before kissing her. He took his time, savouring the sweet taste of her skin, as he tenderly kissed her lips, her neck, her cheeks, her forehead, her eyelids, making her tremble at his touch.

Slipping into an exhilarating daze while struggling to calm her racing heart, the fire was quickly making its way through her body as she opened her eyes, breathless. The look in his eyes at that moment reminded her of that first intense gaze in the bookstore. Honest, blatant desire.

With her eyes intently locked on his, she began unbuttoning his shirt, slowly making her way downward. She gently slid her hands inside, touching the warm soft skin of his chest with her fingers. Inhaling sharply, he responded to her touch as he struggled to control his composure.

She leaned in, lightly kissing his neck as she slowly pulled his shirt over his shoulders and down his arms, caressing his skin as she went. Wrapping her arms around his waist, she continued kissing his neck as he closed his eyes, surrendering to every lingering sensation. His hands moved slowly up and down her back, eventually making their way to her hips and slowly lifting her shirt up and over her head in an effortless fluid motion.

# Behind the Glass

He slowly opened his eyes to quite possibly the most breath-taking sight imaginable as she gingerly removed her bra, seductively locking eyes with him. Marvelling at her beauty, the soft ivory skin of her voluptuous body shimmering in the daylight, literally took his breath away.

Overcome with anticipation, he pulled her close to him by her hips, kissing her deeply as her hands gently caressed his back and broad shoulders. Feeling the heat of her naked skin against his was exhilarating as time seemed to stand still. Having her in his arms like this, feeling her delicate body encompassed by his, he felt utterly whole.

He pulled away for a moment to gaze at her once more, taking in her stunning beauty. She looked back at him with boundless love in her eyes and he knew, with a certainty that only comes once in a lifetime, that this was where he was meant to be.

He gently ran his hands along her sides, over her hips, gently sliding her jeans off as he began kissing her neck. She breathed deeply, letting out the softest moan. She reached for his stomach, ran her fingers downward to the snap on his jeans, undid it, and slowly let them fall to the ground. He pulled her to him by her waist, still kissing her neck, and making his way slowly down to her breasts. She ran her hands wildly through his hair, enjoying the hot touch of his mouth on her body while slipping into a sensual daze.

Unable to resist their deep need for each other for another moment, he pulled her into his arms again, kissing her intensely as they steadily found their way to his bed. Locking eyes with him, she laid back on the bed with her back arched slightly, struggling to control her breathing. Her heart raced as she looked at him above her, overcome with emotion. She marvelled at his beauty as his skin glistened in the sunlight and gently, she reached for his face, pulling him closer to her.

Holding himself only inches above her body, he kissed her softly on the cheek, moving his way slowly down toward her ear. The anticipation she felt throughout every inch of her body was almost too much to bear as he nibbled her ear, exhaling deeply, and driving her wild. Feeling her warm body writhing underneath him, responding to his every touch was insanely arousing.

Unable to control her strength, she pressed her fingers hard into his shoulder blades as she buried her face into his neck, crying aloud as she finally felt him deep inside her. As they joined together as one, with their blood rushing, their nerves overloaded by the constant waves of pleasure washing over them, it was unmistakably the purest sensation of their lives.

He took his time making love to her, enjoying each moment, each breath, each feeling they shared together. Seeing every emotion cross her face as he moved above her, every wave slowly building, every release, and knowing that she trusted him completely to take her wherever he wanted to go only made him want her more.

They moved perfectly in sync, finding their own beautiful rhythm together as if they were the only two people on earth. Everything gradually faded away, leaving nothing else in their private universe but each other. He looked at her as he always had, as if she was the only woman in the world, making her feel truly beautiful, truly sexy and unconditionally... *his.*

They spent the rest of the afternoon making love, alternately holding each other in the peaceful silence as the sun began to fade in the late afternoon sky. The sun shone across the bedroom, casting brilliant sunbeams overhead as he admired her radiant naked body.

The world fell out of focus around her and he knew without a doubt that from this moment on, he would spend the rest of his life making her happy, taking care of her, giving her anything she wanted in this world. From the depths of his heart and his soul, he was hers.

"I love you, Rebecca."

She held his steady gaze, running her fingers gently along his neck.

"I've wanted to say that to you for so long, but I've never actually said the words."

"You didn't have to." She smiled softly and kissed him once, gently on the lips.

"I've always known. You've shown me how much you love me in everything you've said and done since the moment I met you. I've never felt more loved or more wanted in my life."

"Neither have I." He paused, surveying her face slowly with a vulnerable intensity. "You're part of me... deep in my veins. With one look from you, the world stops. All I see is you. All I've ever seen is you. From the first moment I saw you, I have belonged to you. Completely. And I always will. I love you more than you can possibly imagine, Rebecca."

Speechless, her heart jumped as it always had when he looked at her this way, and she silently caught her breath. She reached for his face, pulling him to her, and kissed him deeply. She pulled away gently, still holding his face in her hands.

"I *can* imagine, trust me, I can. I love you so much, Michael."

They held each other for hours in the quiet solitude of their own private oasis, drifting in and out of sleep, feeling nothing in the world but each other's beating hearts and warm embrace. After today, their lives would never be the same. They had always been drawn to one another, but now they were genuinely connected, each unable to imagine or even remember life without the other. From this day on there was no ledge, no falling. Only flying, only each other.

The soft touch of his finger tracing her arm woke her. Rebecca slowly opened her eyes and looked across the room at the fading image of the galloping horse painting hanging on the opposite wall. In the dimming light, it was particularly striking with an almost eerie quality reminiscent of the painting of the three white houses from their first night at the bookstore.

"The horse... why is it alone up here?" she whispered, breaking the silence.

"That's Max. He was my first horse growing up. He was the horse I rode throughout my childhood, the horse I learned everything I know on. I had him until I was well into high school, but he died when I was sixteen. He was incredible, definitely one of a kind. This painting of him was one of the first works of art I really connected with, and poured myself into as an artist. It was an emotional turning point for me."

"I can tell. It's stunning."

"I keep it up here to remind myself of that connection, that inspiration, when I'm in a creative lull." He smiled at her, raising one eyebrow. "Not that I need that with my recent work."

She blushed lightly, smiling. "No, you definitely don't."

"It's easy to paint you. You're the most beautiful thing I've ever seen in my life."

He kissed the top of her head, hugging her tightly. She sighed contently in his arms, feeling like the luckiest woman in the world as flashes of the works of art downstairs filled her mind. Being his muse filled her heart like nothing ever had in her life before now.

She looked at the horse painting again, at its vivid details, at each heartfelt brush stroke.

"It reminds me of the painting of the houses, the one from Behind the Glass. The depth in emotion is similar... at least to me."

The memory of that night flashed in his mind. "I remember."

"Maybe it was just that particular time in my life, but when I looked at it, that scene of those three houses reflected exactly how I had been feeling for weeks. It made me realize how lost and incredibly alone I had been. It may not have been your intent, but that's what I saw."

He stared back at her in awe, as if she had just read his mind.

"*Solitude...* it's the title of the painting. I felt the same way when I painted it."

She appreciated the irony. He had always been able to see through to her every emotion since the day they'd met. It was fitting that through his art she was able to do the same. She kissed him once and looked deeply into his gorgeous brown eyes for a long reflective moment.

"You will *never* feel alone again, Rebecca, I promise you that."

"Neither will you, Mr. Vale."

He smiled widely, admiring her as he gently ran his finger along her jaw line.

"I do love the way you say my name."

# Behind the Glass

She leaned in again, smiling and kissed him softly on the cheek next to his ear.

"Mr. Vale..." she whispered breathlessly, instantly driving him wild.

He pulled her close to him again, clearly enjoying her natural effect on him. He kissed her deeply once more, completely captivated, and never wanting to let her go.

She nuzzled into him, knowing deep in her heart that he was everything she had ever needed, and would ever need. For the rest of her life.

He gently kissed her forehead, knowing how fortunate he was to finally have her in his arms, to finally belong to her. He would never take for granted the long road that led them to one another as he whispered softly into her ear, "One day... I'll call you Mrs. Vale."

# Epilogue

*One year later*

Walking down State Street in Madison, no matter how many times a week or a month Rebecca happened to do it never seemed to get old. As far back as she could remember, it had always been a part of her life; from her childhood visits with her parents, her teenage adventures with her friends, to her more recent memories of her unbelievably happy life with Michael.

And here she was again on another gorgeous spring day, walking down the eclectic pedestrian mall, contently taking in every bit of it as she headed toward Azure to meet Leo. Bustling with activity with its coffeehouses, ethnic restaurants, art galleries, and specialty shops, State Street had its own unique subculture and would always be her home away from home.

*Home.* She smiled to herself as she thought of it.

Home for her now was Vale Ranch with Michael and his family, a place she had grown to love more than anything in the world. It didn't take much time or convincing for her to move there with him and embrace the home and the life that he loved so much. Sharing her life with him came as naturally as breathing, and she now couldn't imagine her life any other way.

# Behind the Glass

Michael, along with his father and uncle, worked for months renovating one of the older unused bunk houses into a modest two-bedroom home for them to live in. As a surprise for her birthday, and so they could create art close to one another, they also converted part of the artist's loft into a fully-functioning dark room for her.

Gradually over the past year, the home they created and their new life together had redefined her perception of an oasis. It was so much more than that. It was everything.

She visited Grace and Ethan on a regular basis at her beloved Behind the Glass, and would periodically offer new photography to display around the shop. Over the past year, her work had been displayed at several art galleries around the state and in Madison, and had quickly gained serious recognition. Dominic, along with another couple of Ethan's colleagues, had eagerly taken her under their wing, showing her the business of becoming a bona fide artist while helping her make a regular income with her art.

It was a difficult decision, one she resisted for months, but quitting her two jobs to go back to school full time at UW-Madison for her BFA in Photography was probably the best she'd ever made. Michael had insisted on helping her financially so she could finish school, but she had never been one to depend on others while pursuing her dreams. After more than a half dozen conversations, they had finally come to a compromise. She would pay for school with the profits from her artwork, along with her own savings, while she lived at Vale Ranch with no expenses to speak of. His chivalry and her independence were each other's favourite qualities, and the biggest bones of contention in their relationship, but it certainly kept things interesting.

She adored living on the ranch with him though, with all of her heart.

It was a drastically different lifestyle than anything she had known before, but after a few months it became an integral part of her new life with him. Waking up with the animals at the crack of dawn, helping Michael and the staff feed, water, and groom the horses, being surrounded by dozens of children of all ages at *all times*, spending time with his amazing family, going on day long rides with him to their secret backyard, and sneaking away together to make love at all hours of the day and night became completely normal. And completely perfect.

They had recently gotten into the habit of taking at least one day for themselves each week, amidst the craziness of the ranch and her classes, to spend some quality time together alone. Most days they would go into Madison to do something fun, while others they would spend at their house snuggled in bed all day, or in their private backyard together enjoying the outdoors.

This past weekend stood out beyond all others.

# Behind the Glass

Wisconsin had just had a particularly harsh winter over the past six months, and was finally seeing a change in seasons, along with a gorgeous spring weekend. Michael and Rebecca packed a picnic lunch, saddled up Piper and Duke, and took a ride out to the family's backyard. After they finished lunch and Rebecca was sufficiently enthralled in a quick photography session, Michael discretely poured two glasses of champagne for them and called her over.

The moment she looked into his eyes she knew something was up and her heart raced.

She walked slowly over to the blanket with her eyes still intently fixed on his as he slowly took the camera from her and placed it on the ground. Her first instinct was to lower herself to sit next to him but something in his eyes told her to stand right where she was as he raised himself to his knees. Her heart felt as if it would beat out of her chest.

He took her hands in his, kissed them gently one by one and began his proposal.

"Rebecca, I was drawn to you before we'd even spoken to one another. It's difficult to put into words, but I knew, deep in my soul, from the moment you walked into my life, that you were *the one*. It wasn't any one thing about you, it was everything. I'd never met anyone like you before, and I thank my lucky stars every day that our paths crossed the way they did at Behind the Glass that night.

"Over the past year, you have made me the happiest man in the world, and I have felt complete in a way I'd never known before. I can't imagine my life without you in it, and I want to spend the rest of our lives making you as happy as you've made me. I want to build a life and a home and a family with you and I want..." He paused, smiling at her with that beautiful piercing smile that always melted her heart. "I want to call you Mrs. Vale. Will you do me the great honour of becoming my wife?"

She said, "Yes," and kissed him almost before he'd gotten the whole question out.

Filled with a giddy excitement that ran through every inch of her body, she gazed down at the gorgeous princess cut diamond ring that sparkled brilliantly in the mid-morning sunlight as she continued her way up State Street. It had only been a few days and she couldn't seem to stop herself from pausing every few minutes to look at it.

She couldn't wait to tell Leo.

They had made an early lunch date at Azure to catch up with each other and to discuss the menu Leo and his staff were preparing for Isabel's upcoming baby shower at his mother-in-law's house next weekend. Rebecca was in charge of arranging everything for the shower, and decided to tie up all of the remaining loose ends today, her one day of the week with no classes. She had a list of State Street related errands, but seeing Leo was definitely the highlight of her day.

# Behind the Glass

Rebecca arrived promptly at eleven to find Leo waiting for her in the rear of the main dining room with a huge smile on his face. The moment they met, he scooped her up into one of his infamous bear hugs, clearly excited to finally see her again.

"Hey, girl! You are definitely a sight for sore eyes. I haven't seen you in weeks!"

Laughing as he placed her back down, she said, "I know, it's been way too long!"

As they both took their seats she realized how much she had missed him over the past few months. He had been so wonderful to her when she needed to cut back on her hours, and extremely understanding when she finally quit her job altogether, promising to come back anytime if they were ever in a pinch. Good help was hard to find, and she was one of the best waitresses they'd ever had.

Smiling as she glanced around the restaurant, she observed the pre-lunch buzz of the dining room. "Well, it looks like you guys are surviving just fine without me."

"Yeah, we're doing alright. I'm still thrilled that you're going back to school, don't get me wrong, but *man,* do I miss seeing your face around here every day. It's just not the same. How's life been treating you at the ranch?"

"It's been..." She subtly leaned forward and rested her chin on the palm of her left hand, revealing the brilliant platinum ring that adorned her ring finger. "... *Really* good."

His eyes widened as he gazed at her hand and the ridiculously happy grin on her face. "Well, I see it has! Congratulations! When did this happen?"

As he gently took her hand to examine the ring, she struggled to contain her excitement and keep an even voice. "This weekend. I was stunned. He managed to keep it completely under wraps and I never suspected a thing. It was just... *amazing.* I think it's still slowly sinking in."

"Come on, Bec, you can't tell me you didn't see this coming. Anyone who's seen the two of you together, even for a second, can tell how crazy in love you are. I'm actually surprised it took him this long!" He winked and shot her a playful smirk as he released her hand.

She was positively beaming as she looked back at him. "I can't explain it, but I can't seem to stop smiling about it, about him, about us. Leo, I've *never* been this happy before."

"You deserve to be, Bec. I've always told you that. And I know exactly what you're feeling right now, *trust me.* Don't you remember how insanely happy I was after I met Isabel? It's crazy what happens when you meet the person you're supposed to be with for the rest of your life. Everything changes. You see the world differently. Priorities shift." He paused, looking uncharacteristically serious for a moment. "I'm so happy for you guys, truly."

"Thanks." She reached across the table and squeezed his hand. "I'm happy for you guys too. Just think, in six weeks you're going to be a dad. To the *luckiest* little girl on the planet."

Smiling widely, he shook his head slowly. "Crazy, right?"

"You'll be a natural. So will Isabel. I can't wait to see you guys become parents. And I can't wait for this baby shower!"

"Well, with you planning it for her, it'll be perfect, I'm sure."

Leo opened the folder he'd brought to the table, and began reviewing the menu with her. They sat together for the next hour enjoying lunch while she described the many silly and completely girly aspects of the shower that she had planned, from the games, to the party favours, to the decorations. She also updated him on her evolving photography career, her latest gallery shows, how her classes were going, and of course, her life at the ranch with Michael.

They easily fell back into the familiar rhythm they had always shared as Leo described how they had been preparing for the baby's arrival, what names they were considering, how gorgeous Isabel was, handling pregnancy like a pro, and how unbelievably excited they both were about becoming parents.

He also briefly filled her in on the latest gossip around town, including Jared and Claire's on-again/off-again relationship. After pursuing her for months, he had finally given up the chase and began dating a hair dresser, an adorable blonde who seemed completely enamoured with him. In typical Claire form, it was enough to attract her full attention, and within days, a would-be one night stand together evolved into months of a surprisingly intense, yet tumultuous, courtship. There was never a dull moment, and it was anyone's guess what their future would hold.

After they finished lunch, Leo hugged and congratulated her again before they parted ways. "It was so good to see you, Bec. And tell that fiancé of yours that I'm planning a hiking trip next month and that I'll be in touch next week, okay?"

Her face flushed at hearing him refer to Michael as her fiancé. "I will, I promise."

This was definitely something she would enjoy getting used to.

She left Azure and headed up State Street toward her next stop, Off the Wall, her favourite little shop for finding one-of-a-kind, hand crafted gifts. She had special ordered a hand-made baby blanket that matched the nursery colours perfectly, made of the softest merino wool she had ever laid her hands on. She couldn't wait to give it to Isabel this weekend, along with the dozens of other fun baby gifts she had collected for her bright pink gift basket.

She soaked in the warm sunlight as she strolled at a leisurely pace, smiling contently. She caught herself gazing down at her beautiful engagement ring again, lost in amorous thoughts of Michael and how he'd made love to her early this morning as the sun rose over the ranch.

Yes, letting the word fiancé sink in and settle around her was going to be extremely easy.

Lost in her own heavenly thoughts for a moment, she finally drifted back to the present, looking up again and running head-on into someone coming out of a restaurant.

"Oh my God, I'm so sorry!" she apologized, embarrassed by her space cadet moment.

"Rebecca?" the man she ran into asked, in a familiar voice.

She stared back at him, stunned at first, and then laughed as she regained her bearings.

"*Brett?* ...Oh... Hi!"

Seriously, what were the odds of that?

"Hey there, sorry about that, I didn't see you there. Are you okay?"

"I'm fine. No, that was *all* me, trust me. I was in my own little world for a minute."

They quickly stepped aside together toward the outdoor seating area of the restaurant to let foot traffic flow again. As they looked at each other, they shared a mutual familiar smile.

"It's good to see you. How have you been?"

Dressed in his usual suit and tie, he looked as handsome as ever.

"I've been good. How are things with you?"

She had imagined being face-to-face with him in her mind several times over the past year, wondering what they might say to each other, and if it would be weird or awkward. To her genuine surprise it wasn't, not at all. If anything, it felt comfortable and totally normal.

"Things are good. Work has been as nuts as usual, but I can't complain. The firm's been growing a lot lately, so it comes with the territory. Each day is 'sink or swim,' I swear."

"You were always good under pressure. I'm sure you're doing just fine."

He smiled. "Yeah, I'm doing alright. How's work with you? I hear you're a showcased, up-and-coming photographer these days." His teasing tone was refreshing.

She returned the smile. "Yeah, I'm getting there, slowly. It's been a wild ride so far, but I'm learning a lot, and taking it one step at a time. It's definitely 'sink or swim' too."

She wasn't exaggerating. As exciting as it was, it felt overwhelming at times.

"Well, I've seen your artwork, Rebecca and it's... just beautiful. I'd say you're swimming just fine." He sounded very sincere and smiled warmly, locking eyes with her.

Imagining Brett in *any* gallery setting was almost perplexing. And humbly touching.

"You have? Thanks... that means a lot."

Appearing a bit reflective, he paused before he spoke again, surveying her face slowly.

"You look happy."

Her heart skipped a beat, thinking of how drastically different her life was now, with Michael. Picturing the quiet, demure girl she once was while they were dating, it was merely a distant shadow of who she had become. It felt like a lifetime ago.

"I am... I *really* am."

She sensed a quiet sadness within him as he looked back at her.

"That's all I've ever wanted for you." He stopped himself, as if wanting to say more.

"Brett... I should have called you."

"No, Rebecca. You don't owe me anything. I understand."

"No, I wanted to call you. I actually have for a long time. The letter you wrote me..."

"... is in the past now. You've moved on. And slowly, so have I. You're with Michael now, and from what Leo's told me, you're very happy together. I can see it in your eyes."

"I am." She paused, focusing on him intently. "But you need to know that what happened between us... wasn't just you. I'm just as much to blame. You need to know that."

"I appreciate you saying that, but you still didn't deserve what happened. I can't change the past, but I can certainly learn from it." He shrugged his shoulders, "It is what it is, and at the end of the day I just hope we can be friends, at least on some level."

She smiled, oddly relieved. "I'd like that."

As she looked at him, she realized she'd witnessed a side of him that she'd never seen while they were dating. He was more serious, more straightforward, and more reflective than he'd ever been. Simply put, he'd grown.

She found herself hoping that he would one day find love, as she had with Michael.

"Are you seeing anyone? If you don't mind my asking."

She blurted it out without thinking and hoped she hadn't overstepped.

"I am, actually. We've been together for a couple months now and it's going well."

"That's good to hear, I'm glad."

Smiling softly, his mood lightened as he thought of her. "We actually met through work. She's an accountant for a competing firm. Our biggest rival actually. We were both presenting to the same potential client and things got... interesting."

"Seriously?" She shook her head, smiling. "Only you!"

"Yeah, well I think I may have met my match."

They both laughed. She was pleased to hear he was with someone and seemed happy.

He glanced down at his watch then back at her.

"Do you have to get back?"

"Yeah, sorry. I've got a meeting in thirty minutes."

"Well, I'll let you get going. It was really nice running into you."

"Quite literally!" he teased, smiling again. "It was good to see you too, Rebecca."

Surprising her, he leaned down and gave her a friendly yet tight hug.

"Take care, okay."

"You too."

As they parted ways, he headed up State Street toward his office, while she crossed the street, toward her awaiting errands. Sighing contently, she was truly amazed at how easy that was – seeing Brett again, and talking to each other like old friends.

She actually hadn't thought of him or their relationship much over the past year, but at this moment, felt as if a huge weight had been lifted. Apparently seeing him again, just knowing that he was happy, gave her the closure she didn't even know she needed.

That chapter of her life was now officially closed.

Focusing on the iconic shimmering glass storefront of Behind the Glass up ahead as she continued walking, she reflected on how far she'd come over the past year and how different she was in every conceivable way. That shy, guarded, uncertain girl from the bookstore had evolved into a happy, confident woman who was completely in love with her life.

Because of him.

And because she finally found the one person in this world that she would gladly jump off a ledge with. Now and forever.

*

# COMING SOON

*Off the Wall*, Kristen Morgen's next novel in the State Street Series, focuses on Charlotte, an outgoing, confident young woman who owns a consignment shop. Charlotte feels like she's finally got her life figured out. Life is good. She has a great family, friends, a fun new boyfriend and her best friend, Addie, whom she's known since second grade.

Addie's older brother, Logan, who is six years her senior, is home for a rare visit from Chicago. He has done his best to stay far away from his family over the years, starting his own construction business and steering clear of his millionaire father's plans for his life and career. A casual reunion for lunch with his sister and her best friend 'Charley,' throws him for a loop.

Sparks will fly and boundaries will be pushed. Logan's world will be turned upside down as he discovers that finding the girl he's long been searching for will push and pull him in ways he never imagined.

www.kristenmorgen.com

A publication by Tamarind Hill Press
info@tamarindhillpress.co.uk
www.tamarindhillpress.co.uk

**TAMARiND HiLL**
**.PRESS**